# TE-KILL-YA SUNRISE

## BOOK ONE: CANARY KEY COZY MYSTERIES

# Patti Larsen

Thanks, Kirstin!

ISBN-13: 978-1-989925-64-5

# CHAPTER ONE

Sunset over the beach was my favorite time of day. Warm breezes from the ocean washed over the sand beneath the red, pink and orange sky, carrying the sounds of laughter and chatter. Better yet, evening brought the bulk of business as my place filled with loud and happy vacationers, sunburned cheeks shining, layered cocktails the favorite choice, while less enthusiastic locals sipped cold beer at the bar. The scent of salt mixed with the delicious offerings from the restaurant's kitchen behind me while I poured the slushy contents of the blender into a wide-rimmed glass, brilliant red of grenadine and fresh fruit heaped under a decorative umbrella and speared strawberry.

The young woman who'd ordered the double shot margarita took it with wide eyes and a thumbs up as she sampled it through the straw, walking back toward her table in the sand on wobbling platform sandals unsuited to the footing. I grinned and moved on to my next order while Pika expertly cracked two bottles of icy beer and slid them across the polished wooden bar toward the waiting men, one of whom watched my last customer on her meandering and hip wiggling path back to her giggling girlfriends.

How I loved Thursday nights on Canary Key. Are you kidding? How I loved every minute.

"Becks, heads up." I pivoted while still pouring, pausing long enough to catch the bottle of bourbon I needed from my co-bartender and star employee. Pika was already on her own next drink before the bottle left her hand, making a nice flip over in the fading sunlight to reflect back the dark tint of the contents in a sparkling show that had the waiting customers gasping and clapping. Because of course, I caught it deftly before free pouring the exact amount I needed for the old fashioned the elderly man in the loud pineapple shirt ordered. Two dashes of bitters—his choice—a splash of water and a sugar cube and he was on his way with a wave and a hearty tip left behind.

I returned the favor when I overheard her need for the spiced rum, Pika already turning when she realized I had it, the pass off smooth and making me grin when more cheering arose at her fancy side catch.

The fact I'd only owned Low Key—the restaurant side—and Off Key—the beach bar attached—for six months hadn't held me back from learning everything I could from Pika. I much preferred leaving the management of the dining side to my amazing staff—all of whom I inherited and got along with, thank goodness. Tending bar had been a passion since I'd done so to pay for college, so I was delighted to go back to it at last. And while the adorable, barely five-foot twentysomething with her anime pigtails and round Asian features might not have looked the part, Pika Sato was the best teacher I could have asked for, not to mention my absolute favorite person to work next to.

Which we did most nights. Sure, I still dropped the occasional bottle with a bow and a flourish as part of the show, but Pika never ever did.

I wanted to be her when I grew up.

"A bottle of champagne, please, and four glasses." I'd taken brief note of the quad of women who'd walked in and grabbed the last beach table a few minutes prior, all about my age or more, likely mid-forties with the perfect makeup, hair and tight dresses that denoted women utterly against advancing age, not one of them with a wedding ring on their fingers. I'd come to recognize cougars when I saw them, noted the way the blonde eyed up the two young men who'd ordered Pika's beers, her fitted cream minidress hugging her gym-tight body. Made me grin all over again, this time in amusement rather than pride. Not that I was judging, because you do you and all that, but I'd had my share of taking strangers home from bars in my twenties. No way I was starting up that nonsense again at forty, even if I was single and always had been.

"Celebrating, ladies?" I turned and fished out a cold one from the lower fridge, peeling the foil. Did my best to showboat as one of them, her lovely dark skin and Indian features stunning in her pale pink dress, rose gold dangling from her ears and wrist, filmed the whole process on her phone, long nails matching her jewelry down to the tiny fake diamonds embedded in the polish.

"We are," another said, hooking arms with the grinning blonde, the depth of her skin in direct contrast with her taller friend, full hips and chest straining against the chocolate brown bandage dress she wore like a queen, full, shining black curls that kind of delightful waterfall mass that had everyone staring.

While the last of them, a slim and smiling woman whose olive skin and almond eyes had been perfectly framed by a precise bob haircut with the most amazingly straight bangs I'd ever seen, gave me an elegant nod, full lips smiling.

"My divorce finally came through," she said, while I popped the cork at that exact moment because I was either that good or that lucky.

They cheered, echoed by most of the rest of the bar, while I filled glasses and passed over the bottle, the women saluting each other before downing their drinks.

"We'll be back," the blonde winked at me, blue eyes vivid under thick lashes, red-painted lips not going to last long if she kept drinking like that.

Not my problem. I had a lineup and more than enough to keep my attention. Not the least of which was the returning vagabond I had learned not to worry about when he decided to take strolls on his own out of the blue.

Case in point. He wound his way around a few tables, accepting pats and nibbles of food from those he passed, all big head and broad shoulders and giant paws, tail wagging slow and casual. The brindle mutt with the giant heart I'd fallen in love with from day one slid under the half door to the bar, settling onto the dog bed I'd installed for him, pausing long enough to slip him the dinner Marta sent down an hour ago from the kitchen with a hopeful look.

"You missed your girlfriend," I said, setting the plate down. He gulped his dinner, though I had every reason to believe he'd already eaten at least two other places, before curling up with a grunt, head on his paws. "You're welcome, Bruno."

His tail thumped as the stray who'd adopted me as much as I'd adopted him sighed contentedly and went to sleep.

The next hour or so settled into a familiar rhythm I'd grown to love and look forward to, taking orders, mixing drinks, rinse and repeat while music from the bar's speakers carried out to the beach and drew in more customers. It helped Off Key was pretty much the only game in town, Canary Key small enough to warrant town status but just barely. And while a couple of other boutique restaurants graced the lovely strip of Florida heaven, the only other place to drink was the pool hall and tourists preferred the beach.

Not that I was complaining.

When the gorgeous woman in the rose gold returned to the bar, I complimented her on her gorgeous dark hair. My own was kind of a plain brown with enough red in it to give me attitude without the freckles.

"Thanks," she beamed. Paused. "There aren't any other beach bars here, are there?" I knew that look on her face, that kind of predatory acquisitiveness I'd felt when I'd first seen this place.

"Nope," I said, going back to mixing. "And I like it that way."

She blinked before laughing. "You're the owner?"

I nodded, knowing I didn't really look the part in my ponytail and minimal makeup, jean shorts and branded t-shirt that was our uniform here at Off Key.

She offered her hand immediately. "Nina Kundu, nice to meet you."

I paused in the midst of my drink mixing—two daiquiris and two tequila sunrises coming up—to wipe my hand on a towel before shaking hers.

"Becks Hogan," I said.

"A fellow entrepreneur," Nina said with a smile. "I love your place, Becks. Great branding and obviously excellent business potential." She was in the industry, huh? "Ever think about franchising?"

I finished off her four drinks with appropriate dressing before shaking my head. "Sorry, Nina," I said. "I have my hands full with this place." I waved at the restaurant behind me to include it. "And this key's town council mandated limited beach businesses, so I'm in a solid position I don't want to risk." Not that I was trying to scare her off or anything, but I wasn't about to make it easy for her to shoulder in if that was on her mind. Then again, more than enough people had tried to set up here, only to be stymied by the local municipality, so I knew I lucked out when Dad's old college friend sold this place to me.

"Still." She winked, dark eyes smiling while she expertly handled the four drinks by herself. "Now that Hannah's finally divorced," the Asian woman did seem pretty happy about it, finishing the bottle of champagne straight from the source, "my friends and I are looking at buying a property here, kind of a retirement community for the sisterhood." That made her laugh. "If it works out, I'll be in touch."

I watched her go, not sure that made me happy to hear. I didn't need a partner or competition, thanks. Sure, business was good, but my plan to pay off my dream investment in ten years would have to be readjusted if she managed to convince the municipality to allow her to move in on my profits.

We'd see. I already had an in with the locals, vetted by Conrad Metter when he'd sold to me, and made friends with local law enforcement, business owners and volunteered with the youth center, which meant I'd become part of the community pretty quickly. A community, happily, that seemed invested in those it called family—adopted or not—and offered a colder shoulder to those who didn't belong.

Nothing to worry about, Becks. Right?

# CHAPTER TWO

The next distraction made up for my darker thoughts, Jasper Dunlop arriving at the bar with a rush of energy and an overabundance of youthful enthusiasm I sometimes found tiring in a forty-one-year-old man who acted like he barely hit twenty. With high fives for some of the locals and a beaming smile that lit up the beach, Jasper swaggered his naturally alluring self to the bar, slipping past Bruno with a soft pat for the dog before helping himself to a beer.

"You're late," I growled at him, though my flashing grin had him shrugging and winking.

"You can't rush perfection, Becks." Half the

beer was gone in two big gulps, his tanned jaw heavy with stubble the women loved, full mouth, perfect white teeth I knew were veneers, deep sea-green eyes and full, dark hair without a trace of gray yet giving him that perpetually youthful Prince Charming of Attractivetown that seemed to make women my age and older go mad with plans to tame him and turn him into the ideal husband. Never mind Jasper would never settle down, not in love or in career choices, his present mishmash of occupations including running entertainment for me at Off Key. He finished his beer and helped himself to the two microphone cases under the bar, laptop tucked under one arm before heading out to the stage area at the edge of the deck. "So don't even try."

His return to the crowd, all six feet and broad shoulders of him, dressed in fitted shorts and a button-up that could have stood one more hole fastened at the top, was met with yet another cheer, Jasper quick to fire up one of the microphones.

"Welcome to Off Key Karaoke!" Apt name, right? Or maybe you haven't hung out at a bar for amateur hour. Lucky you.

I should have brought on another bartender, or a server, though I hated to have anyone on the floor on karaoke night, preferring to manage alcohol service where I could keep an eye on those who were drinking. Having a beach bar meant more precautions, and while I knew, for the most part, my insurance was excellent, the thought of having someone wander off and drown while drunk because I overserved them had me waking up in a cold sweat in the middle of the night at times.

As it was, I could manage just enough attention through orders to note with growing amusement and increasing eye-rolling that Jasper was in fine form. Especially with the four ladies who had now graduated to tequila shots amid their fruity drinks, taking turns wailing out old pop tunes from the 90s and 2000s in singles and groups of two to four, dominating the stage all night. While flirting heavily with my friend, naturally, who flirted right back.

It was easy to tell the blonde was taking the bulk of Jasper's attention. Through the horrific strains of rock ballad after bitter breakup song after one-hit-wonder, Jasper expertly managed the ebb and flow of singers, songs and flirting like a seasoned pro on an Olympic circuit to gold.

Naturally, the crowd ate him up, which meant more sales for me and more work for Pika and me. Not complaining. Nights like this one were why I'd dumped my life in Manhattan, left behind winter and garbage and rats and rude baristas and work in the crime lab for endless summer, sand, sea breezes and the life I'd always dreamed about.

Shouting from the stage caught my attention mid-pour, shaking me out of my drink creation dance with a scowl of irritation. While Jasper seemed front and center, he was a lover, not a fighter, and the woman going after the blonde and her friends seemed more than enough of the latter for all of them. It was her shrieking I'd heard, that had everyone turning to look, falling silent enough I caught a few choice swears.

I was already heading for the side hatch out of the bar to break up the impending fight when the smaller woman, her long, reddish hair swinging in soft curls around her, spun and marched off on her own, the blonde lunging for her, only to be held back by Jasper and her friends. I won't repeat the selection of four-letter descriptors the blonde used to describe her departing enemy, but they were strong enough to sizzle in the cooling night air.

I hesitated, saw the four women settle even as I texted for backup. The giant mound of manhood who emerged from the restaurant to wander through the crowd, his tight white logoed t-shirt bearing the Low Key logo on the back, nodded his shaved head to me, Ox Clinton's flat expression hiding the sweet and lovely man he was behind the looming threat his very presence managed without effort.

That settled things down without me having to bounce the drunk women who seemed to have let go of the intruder's interruption and were back to dancing and singing and teasing Jasper, so I returned to bartending, though on alert now and ready just in case.

Part and parcel with the business, though my least favorite. I didn't mind drunks. They came with the territory. But if they brought drama into my bar? They were out and no second chances.

As I hefted the bottle of vodka I'd set down a moment before, I noted a man had perched at the edge of the bar and was staring at the women. Not in a good way or admiring. But with the kind of intensity and frowning focus that had me noting his attitude and taking stock of him. Average looking, dark brown hair mostly gray, with a squinting frown and faint sunburn of someone from a colder clime, he sipped a beer only absently, like he required an excuse to sit there and watch them. Whatever he had to do with the divorced foursome, I was at zero tolerance with the situation now and would call Ox in if needed.

Funny how old instincts kicked in, intuition stronger than ever. I could usually spot trouble, and while I knew the women were going to be a handful, this guy had potential for danger written all over him.

The thing about trouble? It doesn't tend to go away because you want it to. And adding alcohol to the mix? Let's just say I was happy I had muscle floating around.

Because within ten minutes of the first shouting match, another broke out. This time, I was out the hatch and on my way to the stage before I could think about it, Ox bee-lining toward Jasper, the two of us triangulating on my friend who did his best to get between the shouting blonde—her again—and a tall, bald man who did his best to get to her past Jasper.

"Enough," I said, Ox stopping next to me in almost perfect lockstep. The newcomer looked at me with a scowl of disdain but paid attention when his gaze traveled up and over my shoulder. I might not have looked intimidating, but Ox certainly did. The giant scar he'd gotten as a kid from falling off his bike, the one that ran from his chin to his forehead on a diagonal that gave him a perpetual sneering scowl helped a lot, too, along with his six-foot-six linebacker physique and fists the size of ten-pin bowling balls.

You think I'm joking. There was a reason we called him Ox.

"Go away!" Blondie was very drunk at this point hanging off Jasper and shouting with trembling fury at the now cowed man beside me. "Leave me alone, Melrose!"

"We need to talk, Sunny," Melrose snarled, checked himself. Tried for calm and almost made it under the weight of Ox's attention. "I know you cheated. I'm taking you back to court and I'm going to have the prenup challenged."

"You lost the right to talk to me about anything," she shot back, "when we got divorced." She tossed her head, shining hair shimmering around her while her girlfriends glared at Melrose down their noses in a line of disapproval so obvious I almost chuckled. And might have if they weren't making my bar the center of their spectacle. So bad for business.

"You," I snapped at him, jabbing at the exit with my index finger. "Consider yourself barred." He glared, mouth opening to protest. "Before you say a word, let's keep that to just barred and not incarcerated for the evening. I have the police chief on speed dial and I'm not afraid to call her." He still hesitated, glaring at the blonde he'd called Sunny. "Allie Crown loves nothing more than to toss errant tourists into a jail cell for the night for disturbing the peace." I was bluffing, of course. Allie would kick me in the butt if she knew I was using her as a weapon. What she didn't know would make her ears burn.

My shut down had a different influence on the

women. They cheered and jeered, Ox moving behind me to put himself physically between Melrose and his ex-wife. Which had me all the more unhappy to be out here, on the floor, dealing with this and not serving at the bar in nice, happy contentment. They were harshing my personal buzz that had only surface attachment to alcohol. "You four," I spun on them since it was their turn, "no more drama or you're next. Got me?"

They all nodded and came forward to hug me and thank me in tipsy delight while Jasper fired up the music again. I really loved my life, my job, my bar. Only occasionally did it make me wonder what I'd gotten myself into. Being hugged by drunk and grateful strangers?

Still took getting used to.

## CHAPTER THREE

I took note of three things as I headed back to my place behind the bar at last. One, that Ox had returned after delivering the ex-Mr. Sunny to the street and stood watch over the women like the most excellent and prized employee he was (who'd be seeing a nice bonus in his next check if he kept them from causing any more problems). Two, the original creeper lurking and watching them hadn't moved and continued his observation of them with that same dark, steady stare that almost had me calling said amazing bouncer to come and take care of more business for me, holding Ox in reserve just in case.

And three? Pika was not only holding her own, she'd shifted into overdrive and was just serving the last of the customers at the bar when I joined her again, perky head tilt and wide-eyed cartoon makeup that transformed her heart-shaped face into something unearthly under the fringe of perfect bangs and bubblegum bright eyeshadow.

"All good, *bosu*," she said with a wink and a grin of her shining pink lips, reapplying another coat on her gloss though they didn't need them before rapidly and expertly restocking the beer fridge from the stacked cases under the bar. While I favored jean shorts, she was all about the cute, flared skirts and suspenders and adorable white sneakers with knee socks in rainbow stripes. From her dangling fox earrings to her porcelain complexion, Pika reminded me far more of a Japanese pop star slumming it at my place than a morgue attendant and local ME assistant who loved to moonlight at Off Key. I was just grateful her lifetime spent working at her parent's restaurant in Miami meant she handled herself better than bartenders I'd met twice her age and loved it as much as I did.

We fist-pumped, elbow bumped, and, on her insistence, hip bumped before clapping once and getting back to work.

I really did love it here.

The ruckus had done nothing to slow the intake

of alcohol from my clientele, which meant I barely looked up again but for the occasional check-in with Jasper and Ox to make sure things were civil and the guests happy from then until just before 1AM and closing time. I'd pushed the local municipality to allow me to keep the doors open after midnight Thursday through Saturday and won despite griping from the occasional resident resenting the noise, so I had to be sure things stayed respectful and any fights or excess drama curtailed. No way was I losing that extra three hours a week. While it might not seem like much, I could bank more in that short time period than I did most Mondays altogether, at least on the bar side. Having Low Key close at eleven urged those not yet ready to go home just yet to have a beer or two on the beach and that suited me just fine.

I didn't get to say goodnight to Jasper, the boxed microphones and laptop returned by Ox who nodded toward the laughing women exiting. And who do you think the blonde one called Sunny hung off as he guided her with expert hands and a winning smile toward the parking lot?

Oh, Jasper, you dog.

I wasn't about to tell my friend how to live his life since he'd made it obvious from the day we'd met he'd never change and that the game was one of the great joys of his carefree and childishly selfish existence. Don't get me wrong, he was a good guy and all, would never hurt anyone on purpose, and was always upfront about what he wanted. At least, that's what he told me, and I had no reason to doubt him. But that kind of lifestyle had to take a toll eventually, didn't it?

What did I know? I settled empties into the box in front of me and stacked a load into Ox's arms to be carried back to Low Key for storage and return the next day, happy I'd never fallen for Jasper's charms. I don't think I could have stayed friends with him if I had, and I really liked having him around.

As I moved to fill the next box, however, my worries for my friend went from the usual to the more threateningly immediate as the lurking watcher who'd lingered over two whole beers all evening finally stood, tossing cash on the bar and following with a deep scowl on his face. You better believe I texted my friend the moment I noticed, anxiously checking my cell as I swiped, wiped and closed up.

I finally got a message back while I was lowering the wooden shutters to block off the bar from the beach, Jasper's cheerful, *Thanks, Becks!* so like him I had to sigh. Well, I tried. If he got the crap beaten out of him thanks to a jealous boyfriend or something, that was on him now.

Ox had removed the tables and chairs from the sand, the exterior bar space now empty as it was every night, the deck and front of the bar with its built-in stools exposed but the rest hidden away behind the clever dropdown panels that closed off the important parts to the public. While setup was a bit of work every day, it was worth it to be able to spread out on this stretch of beach and take advantage of the gorgeous sunsets that lured patrons to my bar as much as the alcohol did.

"See you tomorrow!" Pika grabbed her pink unicorn backpack and bopped out, ear pods blasting Japanese pop music so loud I could hear it, too, Ox walking her to the parking lot. Not that he needed to. I watched them go with a grin, knowing the lumbering bouncer had a crush on my young friend and that she never even looked at him except to wave hello.

Also none of my business. I was the last person who should be handing out relationship advice. They'd both grown up here on Canary Key, so his fascination and her utter lack of recognition was hardly something I had history or insight into.

Why then did I feel so badly for the big lug?

With a sigh that was half-amused, half worried about my adopted family, I turned to the giant dog now looking up at me from his cushion with that serious look on his goofy face.

"I know," I said, tossing him a strawberry which he ate in one gulp, no chewing. "Don't look at me like that. I'll mind my own business, promise."

Bruno was the kind of wise, old dog who'd been around the block way more than I had. Maybe that's why he always behaved like he knew exactly what I was saying to him. And right now? He didn't look like he believed me.

That was on him.

# CHAPTER FOUR

It wasn't until the cash was counted out, the night's deposit added to the one from the restaurant, and the next day's float prepped and ready in the safe in the main office at Low Key that I was ready to go. Bruno followed me when I left the bar to finish up, padding his way on my heels, head low, sleepy still but ever faithful. He waited for me by the door when I locked up the main entry and headed for my Jeep, the brightly painted wrap advertising Low Key and Off Key making me shake my head at what I'd been thinking. Then again, the fact it stood out in bright pinks and yellows and greens and blues was kind of the point.

It caught attention and got me business, so despite feeling very obvious in it, I stood behind the decision.

Bruno heaved himself up into the back, taking up the full spread of the bench seat in the rear, leaving me to drive. I'd taken the top off this morning after a hard rain, the clear night sky promising another gorgeous day in paradise tomorrow. Jacked up chassis, oversized knobby tires and all, I rumbled out of Low Key's parking lot like I owned the place.

Which I did. *Yee*-haw.

The bank's exterior lighting always made me feel safe, even when doing deposits on my own, though knowing I had Bruno with me always increased the odds in my favor. Never mind my years playing volleyball in college, the kung fu training I'd taken during my years as a New York City forensics tech, or the fact my dad had been an Olympic gold medal boxer who made sure his oldest daughter knew how to throw a punch. Not that I went looking for trouble, don't get me wrong. That same dad died from a bullet wound he took as a beat cop trying to be a hero—hey, it was his job, I know that but still, I wanted my dad back even now twenty-five years later—so I wasn't about to make myself a target. If I wasn't so comfortable with the key and the residents, the fact that everyone had each other's backs around here, I might have waited until morning or brought someone from the staff with me.

As it was, I made my deposit and was back in the Jeep, bouncing for home on the robust suspension in under a minute. A text came through, and though I'd never type and drive, I did check the sender. Mom had moved to Hawaii with her new husband shortly after my youngest sibling and only brother, Gray, moved out, so I didn't get to see her much. She'd kind of fallen apart after dad died, leaving me to pick up the pieces at fifteen. Which meant my own hopes for the Olympics died when I had to get a job to help keep us going long enough for Mom to pull herself together.

No resentment. Dad taught me well enough for that, and it was just volleyball and more his dream than mine. A lot died with him that night, I had to admit, though I never let go of this particular desire and was so glad I'd hung on through all the years I wondered and worried and did my best for my family.

*Still up*, she sent. *Call me if you have a minute.*

Mom knew I kept late hours. It made it easy for us to talk, actually, and I looked forward to our chats. Funny how distance made us closer than we'd ever been, that this last six months of talking every other night while my day was ending after midnight and hers just really winding down five hours behind me.

I pulled over long enough to send her a quick message back. *Just heading home now*, I sent. *I'll check in shortly.*

*I have news*, her text arrived right after mine, which meant she'd been typing away in her slow and methodical old lady method that made me laugh but got the job done. *Your brother is getting married!*

Huh. I stared down at the phone screen with a little lurch in my stomach. Gray? To me, he was still a skinny, sweet kid with a giant laugh and permanently bandaged knees from falling when he ran, who loved bugs and begged for pancakes for supper and loved video games over everything else. No way my scrawny, funny, adorable baby brother grew up, became a military analyst with our stepfather's private security firm, and was now getting *hitched*.

*Rhea is going to call you*, Mom went on as I sat frozen, the Jeep's motor humming in anticipation of our departure, the headlights shining down the main street, quiet and empty of traffic. *She wants to arrange for us to meet early so we can do a little family thing before the wedding.*

My high-powered lawyer sister with her judge for a husband, perfect twin daughters and fist around the neck of the justice system in Manhattan would want that. I know the first child was usually the A-type alpha, but I'd somehow missed that particular designation. My sister Rhea, on the other hand, had grasped it in an iron grip of dominance and forced life to take her seriously and give her everything she wanted. Or else.

*Okay, Mom.* There was no use in arguing. It would be what it was. I looked up with a sigh, inhaling the humid Florida night, the scent of the ocean so close but out of sight, skin damp from the lingering heat of the day, knowing I smelled like spilled booze and salt and Bruno. Stared up at the giant full moon that rose over the tree line just past the library as one last text came in.

*Love you, honey*, Mom sent. *I miss you.*

*I miss you, too.* I tossed my phone to the passenger's seat and pushed the Jeep into gear, driving home with mixed feelings I hadn't expected. I should have been happy for Gray, that I'd get to spend some time with my siblings and my mother. Celebrate my baby brother's wedding with the ones I loved.

Why then did it sound like the worst possible way to spend a few days of my life?

Funny how you can get wrapped up in thinking about something and totally forget where you are and what you're doing. You know when you suddenly snap out of it and realize you've been driving on autopilot? That moment happened for me at the intersection outside the Sunrise, Sunset Hotel just off Main, and only because I had to brake for a red light.

Which meant, as I came back to myself, I was in the perfect position to see none other than Jasper Dunlop standing outside on one of the top floor balconies, kissing the blonde woman, Sunny.

While someone watched from the shadows below.

# CHAPTER FIVE

I parked without a second thought in the small lot across the street, the flower shop long closed for the day and its single light near the front door giving me the cover I needed to slip out of the Jeep and hurry across the street to the hotel, keeping the watcher in my sights the whole time.

I know what you're thinking, so don't even bother saying it. Of course, it was a stupid idea to go after whoever it was—though I had a good idea I already knew thanks to the bar situation—on my own, no weapon or badge, though I did have a giant dog pacing beside me and ready to defend me at a moment's notice. Maybe if my dad taught me to step aside and let other people handle things? I might have had a different reaction. But daughter or not, I was his firstborn and I bore the brunt of his honor code to this day.

I was surprised when Jasper and Sunny disappeared into the room upstairs by the time I reached the other side of the street, even more so to finally identify the watcher when the man stepped out into the light. Not the same one from the bar at all, but a vaguely familiar face, though if I'd met the Latino in the dark blue work pants and shirt who stuck his hands in his pockets and hurried off with his head down now that the show was over, I couldn't place him.

I'd barely reached the spot where he'd stood for his voyeuristic lingering when none other than my friend and his evening's entertainment emerged from the hotel's front door, laughing and chatting as they climbed into Jasper's small, red convertible and zipped away. Heading in the direction of his apartment, so maybe they'd had no luck finding privacy here if all the friends were sharing rooms.

Letting a one-night stand know where you live wasn't the safest choice, but I was thinking like a woman.

I'd just turned to head back across the street when Bruno growled, low and threatening, warning me to stay in the shadows. With one hand on the thick, leather collar I'd bought him, I watched as he did, ears perked, while the man from the bar made an appearance. This time he oozed from out of darkness of his own by the front entry bushes, only to sneak inside. To what end? I had no idea, but I didn't like the look of it one bit.

At least Jasper was safe. That was all that really mattered. It seemed their stalker hadn't caught up with them and hopefully wouldn't. Waffling over what to do, I finally shrugged into the night air and returned to my Jeep, driving home after sending yet another text to my philandering buddy. No response this time. Just like Jasper.

I made one last stop five minutes from home, the gas station pump chugging to fill my big tank, Bruno now perched in the front seat, sitting up as tall as any human, panting and watching me with interest.

"No treats," I said. "You're getting chunky now that you're living the easy life."

He yawned at me with a rumbling protest wrapping up the jaw-cracking, teeth flashing expression, slow tail wag thudding against my upholstery.

And wouldn't you know? Another familiar face made an appearance, though this person wasn't someone I'd hoped to see again since I'd had him kicked out of my bar. But if Sunny's ex-husband,

Melrose, noticed me at all, he made no indication of it, pulling up at the next pump and filling his own tank while—hello there, drama—the woman who'd assaulted Sunny earlier got out of the passenger's seat and headed for the store inside. Canary Key was a small place, granted, but not usually this small.

She emerged quickly, a bottle of vodka in her hands. "It's all they had, Mel," she said as she came in earshot.

"Just get in the car, Chrissy," he snapped back, jerking at the handle and replacing his gas cap with aggressive force.

The two climbed in and drove off, heading in the direction of the hotel, back the way I'd come, passing curiosity washed away by a massive yawn of my own.

"I really hate drama," I told the dog.

"Woof," Bruno replied. Clearly, he still struggled to believe me. And since drama seemed to be finding me a lot in the last few hours—work and personal—maybe he was right to doubt.

"You're smarter than most people I know." I topped off my tank, suddenly wiped out and ready for bed at last. "Let's go home, buddy."

Morning meant a to-do list a mile long, though I didn't mind. Hands full, I barely noticed as Bruno hopped down and raced off, his day of solo adventures ahead of him and no longer attempting to curtail his sense of freedom. When I'd adopted him, a rangy mutt in terrible need of a vet and good food, he'd been a sort of mascot of the other businesses on the beach, but no one took responsibility for him. Begging had been his primary source of nourishment, along with garbage can vandalism. When I caught him trying to hop up into one of my kitchen dumpsters, we'd had a showdown that ended with him wagging his tail and rolling over so I could pat his belly and me sighing and taking him home.

When I tried to leave him there, however? He managed to do enough damage to my house I finally agreed to let him come with me every day. Which meant getting used to him wandering off to live his best doggy life on his own terms while I did my thing. Worked for both of us though sometimes I was tempted to put a camera on him to see where he went.

With the restaurant already halfway through breakfast, I skirted the main dining area, nodding to my day manager, Juliette Rivers, who grinned and waved a coffee pot back, before ducking into the office to deliver the list of needed items I'd been emailed for the morning. That job done, I headed for the bar and stock taking, knowing I had a liquor store run to make before I opened for the day.

The sound of Bruno barking lured me out into the sand, paper and pen in hand with half a list finished, to find him nudging someone sitting on one of the stools I'd had permanently affixed to the bar. I recognized the woman immediately, her head down on the wood, arms dangling, her cream dress and discarded shoes easily recognizable, purse tipped over at her bare feet, contents scattered across her sand-filled heels.

Great, she'd passed out at my bar. Which led me to wonder where the heck Jasper had gotten to. While I approached and touched her shoulder with the intention of waking her gently. Only to have her topple sideways to the sand, rolling over onto her back as she did, milky eyes gazing upward at the clear, blue sky.

However she'd ended up here, it didn't end as she'd intended unless being dead had been the goal of her evening. Not the worst part as far as I was concerned, though, I'm not ashamed to admit it. Even as I reached for my phone to call Canary Key's chief of police, I winced. Because she had to die at my bar, right? And the last person I'd seen the corpse with?

Jasper Dunlop. Just freaking lovely.

# CHAPTER SIX

Police Chief Allie Crown nodded as she recorded everything I said on her phone, maintaining eye contact with her gray-blue gaze steady and calm, sandy blonde hair shining in the morning sunlight, shot with enough silver at the temples it sparkled when she moved. Perfectly matched at my own height of 5'7", she and I had always literally and figuratively seen eye-to-eye, right from the moment we'd first met. Whether it was the fact I'd come from law enforcement myself, or that my dad was a cop, or we just clicked, Allie had been an instant friend I could count on no matter what.

This event was no exception, the chief arriving less than five minutes after I called her, no sirens or kerfuffle, bless her, keeping the truth on the down-low as long as she could. Sure, I know she did it mostly to prevent locals from interfering before she could get a handle on the situation, but I also chose to believe she did so to protect me and Off Key from bad press as much as possible.

The fact her quarter-ton truck with the shining Canary Key Police Department logo was parked in my lot that early wouldn't mean much to passersby, either, considering our friendship was common knowledge, so I had some breathing room to focus on filling her in rather than worrying about the impact a death on my property would have. I ignored the two mounted cops riding past me on the beach, the hunched and white-overalled Monroe County ME, Dr. Carter Wilson, who'd shown up only shortly after Allie herself. I even avoided eye contact with my own Pika Sato in matching less-than-glam blue plastic booties and marshmallow full zip aiding the doctor. Any other time, I would have taken a moment to say hello, talk shop, since I had intimate knowledge of their present activities. Instead, I felt myself closing off, compressing into intense attention to Allie, only peripherally aware of the various officers Allie brought with her to secure the scene. All in favor of doing what I knew was required of me thanks to a decade and a half on the job. Which meant I shook off my discomfort—not with the death, I'd seen enough of that, but with the tenacious attachment said death had to my bar—and finished telling her everything I knew. Yes, including who I'd last seen with the victim. And no, that didn't make me a traitor, I swear. Remember I said Canary Key was small?

If I didn't spill, Allie would just find out anyway.

The chief sighed at Jasper's name but didn't interrupt further, shifting her weight from one shining black boot to the other, navy blue uniform pristine, the radio on her shoulder turned down to a mild squawk, white t-shirt just showing at her collar a sharp contrast to her deep tan. I'd been around cops my whole life, but aside from my dad, I'd never felt so comfortable and confident as I did with Allie Crown. Which should have made this easier.

So why didn't it? I guess because my life and dream had never been on the line like this before. Now I knew how the victims of the crimes I investigated felt, I guess.

"Thanks, Becks." She shut off her recording and pocketed her phone, squinting at the unfolding investigation carried on by her people and Carter.

"Sorry, but I'm going to have to keep you closed until this is sorted."

I did my best not to show my unhappiness. I'd already waved off Juliette twice since telling her to close up quietly and ask the present patrons to leave without Allie having to ask because it was hardly a surprise the chief made the request. I wasn't a cop's daughter for nothing. Still, the loss of revenue hurt. Friday revenue, no less.

Hey, you try running your own business with profit margins as tight as they came and not make everything about money.

"I get it," I said. "Let me know if you need anything." I was about to finally fill in my staff when Carter straightened from his examination of the body and turned toward us, leaving Pika to finish up while he approached.

Which meant my intention to make myself scarce went out the window because dressed like a giant marshmallow from head to toe or not, Carter Wilson was too delicious a visual snack to walk away from.

What, did you think I was a nun or something?

He pushed back his hood, short, black hair glossy in the sun, those sea-green eyes rimmed in the longest, thickest lashes I'd ever seen. Any other woman would be jealous of those eyes. I was just happy to admire them, along with the full-lipped and perfectly white smile he offered, grim or not, the faint stubble on his tanned jaw with that perfect cleft in the middle of his square chin that had me staring. Big hands stripped the blue latex gloves from his hands as he towered over us at an easy 6'2", surprisingly warm and expressive tenor voice dipping just to baritone as he spoke.

"Hi, Becks." He nodded to me first, bless his gorgeousness, before addressing Allie. And no, I didn't miss the hot and fast grin she shot me at the fact. "Al."

"Thanks for coming so quick, Carter," Allie said, fists on hips, all casual like she hadn't just made me blush with her knowing look. Good thing she wasn't into men, or I'd have to fight her over the gorgeous doctor.

Who was I kidding? I had the entirety of the key and likely the bulk of Monroe County in line ahead of me, so it wasn't like I had much of a chance anyway. Didn't mean I couldn't admire him. The man was delish.

He tucked the used gloves into his pocket through the slit in his suit, unzipping it to reveal a white t-shirt beneath. "Just luck I drove down yesterday," he said. Oh, how I loved it when he stayed at his weekend place here on the key. It meant he'd be by the bar every night and give me some eye candy to enjoy. While not an every week occurrence, it happened often enough I looked forward to Friday through Sunday for more reasons than just my increase in income. "You'll be wanting more than I have for you at the moment."

"I know," she waved his words off with a tight grin. "You don't like to jump to conclusions on site." Was I wrong I felt suddenly jealous of their work relationship? Yes, Becks. Yes, it was. "Just give me what you're comfortable with and we'll go from there."

He was about to respond when commotion from the entry to the bar broke out, three familiar women appearing and trying to push through the pair of officers holding the line. We all gave them attention before I spoke over their demanding and loud voices.

"That's her friends," I said, their more casual attire still above the t-shirt and shorts average of regular tourists to Canary Key. The fact not one of them looked hungover surprised me.

"Noted," Allie said, motioning for the officers to let them through. They charged onto the scene, past the already bagged body now hefted onto a gurney, ready for transport to the county's plain white medical examiner van parked just to the right of the entry, unobtrusive despite the small Monroe County ME logo on the front door. The three stopped in front of us, Nina Kundu speaking for all of them at volume.

"Your deputy wouldn't tell us anything," she said, hands on hips matching Allie's, a woman obviously accustomed to getting her own way. "What's going on? Why did you ask for us to meet you at your office?"

"There's been an… incident." Allie glanced at Carter who nodded. "I'm afraid I have bad news. Your friend, Sunny Thicker, died last night."

They all stared, silenced by the truth. When the gorgeous woman with the massive head of black curls spun on Carter, I jumped to an immediate conclusion that was proven right as she addressed him.

"Dr. Latoya Harper," she said. Carter shook her offered hand.

"Dr. Carter Wilson." He let her fingers go a moment later while my traitor brain wished I'd been the one touching him. Weird, I know, but it had been a minute since I dated anyone, let me tell you, and he really was that hot.

Becks, come on.

"You're the ME?" Latoya obviously knew her way around the lingo, at least.

"I am," he said. "I'm very sorry for your loss."

She waved that off, and, to my surprise, I realized none of the women had shed a tear as yet. In fact, they still looked stunned, but far from grieving. Maybe it would kick in later? Seemed like an odd reaction to me, though.

"Do you know what happened?" The slim woman with the stunning almond eyes hugged herself, at least, showing some distress if not the level I'd been anticipating. She offered her hand to him, too, then to Allie. "Dr. Hannah Chang, psychology." She shrugged. "So easy on the jargon, please, Dr. Wilson."

He shook his head, again deferring to Allie. "Chief Crown can fill you in once I've delivered my report. Again, I'm so sorry for your loss."

"Was she murdered?" That came from Nina Kundu, the entrepreneur turning to stare at the departing gurney while I winced at the sight of a gathering crowd. Word had gotten out after all, likely because Low Key was closed, though any chance of keeping this a secret in a local population of a little over seven thousand people before tourists was slim to none anyway.

Carter's hesitation had Allie stepping in, arms now wide, corralling the women and guiding them aside with a nod to one of her officers. "We don't have enough information yet," she said, pausing just within earshot.

"Oh my god." Hannah finally burst into tears, though she restrained them quickly, Latoya hugging her with one arm, Nina shaking her head, hands trembling as she ran them through her long, dark hair.

"This is crazy," she whispered at the sand before looking up, dark eyes huge. "Have you found that guy she went home with last night?"

I winced at what amounted to an accusation, but Hannah interrupted immediately.

"We all know who killed Sunny," she whispered in a hoarse croak that silenced all three women while the therapist pulled herself together enough to lift her tear-filled gaze to Allie. "Her ex-husband," she said, voice stronger. "Melrose Lewis killed her, and we all know why."

# CHAPTER SEVEN

Now, Carter hadn't confirmed murder, but Allie didn't seem to think it much of a reach when she simply nodded and waited for the woman to go on.

But it was Nina Kundu who did so in Hannah's place, index and thumb of her right hand sweeping over her own left ring finger as though missing the metal that used to live there. "He showed up out of the blue last night," she said. "The divorce was over a year ago, and he's still badgering Sunny." She flinched then, looked away. "She said he'd threatened her in the past, but none of us thought he'd go through with it." I knew guilt when I saw it, Nina glancing at her friends who stared back in mute horror. "We should never have let her go off with that guy."

Which now had me very worried about Jasper, though I didn't get to pipe up and ask about him before Allie did.

"Anyone seen Jasper Dunlop since last night?" The cool, professional way she asked startled me. Wait, did Allie really think he could have hurt someone? No way, not in a million years. Not Jasper. Sure, I'd only known him six months, but I prided myself in being an excellent judge of character. I had no illusions about his or the fact he was a selfish man-child with a penchant for clinging to activities more acceptable in much younger men. But a killer? I'd drink Off Key dry if that proved true.

I had to get ahead of this. "I ran into Melrose Lewis early this morning." I'd failed to tell her because, quite frankly, I'd forgotten all about the encounter until now. Allie turned to meet my gaze, her own flat and the barest bit unhappy, but I wasn't about to let her suspect Jasper when the ladies were probably right about Sunny's ex-husband. "He was getting gas, around 2AM." I nodded to the women. "That other chick was with him. Chrissy?"

That had them all staring in renewed shock,

though Latoya's snort and sudden anger shifted them all to bitter frustration in a flash.

"Of all people," she snarled.

"Why would he be with Chrissy?" Hannah seemed the only one whose ire was mixed with worry. But why would she be concerned her friend's ex was with her, well, ex-friend?

"Melrose has been a horror show since Sunny filed for divorce." Nina seemed confident in the suspect's guilt, glazing over the mention of Chrissy with a wave of one hand. "He blamed her for losing everything."

"Except he was the one caught cheating," Hannah nodded, leaning into Latoya. She sounded like she was repeating something she'd said a million times in her head. "Their prenup was clear."

The three nodded in unison, like that was some kind of mantra, as they all repeated, "He cheated. The prenup was clear."

"You don't say." Allie shot me a look that told me to keep my mouth shut this time or move on, so I held my ground and silence as Hannah went on in a dazed tone of voice.

"Sunny got everything," she whispered. "The house, her practice, their investments. She drafted the prenup, so she knew what she was doing."

More group nodding.

"He's been struggling," Nina said then, with that same crisply accusatory way of hers. "We all knew it. The fact he showed up here, last night when we were all finally free?" She shrugged as though to shed any other supposition in the face of logic and her own personal judgment. "He was always jealous."

"That's why he agreed to the prenup," Hannah said, voice low and trembling.

Nina frowned at her friend but went on, authoritative CEO persona firmly in place as she swept one hand in front of her as though wiping clean the slate of doubt forever. "If he saw Sunny leave with that man, there's an excellent chance he would have lost it completely and just..." She bit her full lower lip, trailing off instead of finishing the obvious.

Okay, now I was really worried about Jasper. Almost reached for my phone to text him. Held off when I realized Allie was watching. What, to see if I did just that? This was a new side to her I'd never encountered before and I wasn't liking being under scrutiny, not one bit.

I hardly blamed her, and yet. Sheesh, we were friends, all of us. She knew Jasper better than that. Wait, did this mean I wasn't as good a judge of people as I thought I was? Or was I jumping on bandwagons because of loyalty and a need to trust those I called family?

Wouldn't be the first time. But it would be if one of those I believed in really was a murderer.

"What about Chrissy?" Allie looked back and forth between the three. "Her full name?"

"Christina Younger," Nina spoke up immediately.

"We were friends once," Hannah said.

"Not anymore," Latoya said as though that ended the conversation.

It didn't. Allie waited patiently enough for them to go on, the silence so achingly painful by the time Nina spoke again I felt my own lips trembling to say something, anything, to end the awkward pause. A tactic, I knew, cops were very good at, but that never made me feel any better about it.

"She's unimportant," Nina said.

"I'll be the judge of that." Allie's steady attention finally seemed to shake the businesswoman who nodded and looked away. "Did any of you notice anyone watching you last night?" The chief was at least taking the information I gave her seriously. But when each of them shook their heads in authentic surprise after exchanging looks, Allie let it rest. Not that I could. What if the man at the bar killed Sunny and did something horrible to Jasper? "I'm going to ask you to go with my officers." She waved to the pair who had helped Pika with the body and now hovered, waiting for orders. They came immediately forward to do their boss's bidding while the three women glanced their way, equally anxious expressions arising at the approach. "I just have a few more questions and I think you'll all be more comfortable out of the hot sun."

"Do we need to call our lawyers?" Nina certainly had her head on straight.

Allie's head tilt and faint smile were known to disarm, but I knew better. "I don't know, Ms. Kundu," she said. "Do you?"

The officers led the three friends away, Nina glancing back with a scowl at Allie, while my friend turned her back on the departing trio and fixed me with a stern stare.

"I know you're worried about Jasper," she said, holding up one hand as I attempted to protest, "but so am I, okay? I'm doing my job, Becks."

Carter spoke up before I could respond, apparently appearing contrite enough Allie didn't push the matter.

"Your instincts may or may not be correct," he said. "I found evidence of strangulation, though whether it was consensual or the cause of death I have no idea." He managed it so casually I caught myself blushing. Far from a prude, something about the way he said it had me feeling like a fourteen-year-old looking at dirty photographs for the first time.

Movement at the edge of the perimeter caught my eye when I looked away to cover my flushed reaction, the sight of the Latino man in the blue work clothing registering after a second of confused recognition. Wait, wasn't that the same man I'd seen at the hotel, the one I thought I knew from somewhere? But my attempt to alert Allie had to wait because a moment later the guy who'd been hanging out at the bar last night—the very guy my friend just asked about—strode through the barricade and headed right for us, flashing a badge at the Canary Key chief, ignoring Carter and me completely as he did.

"Detective Thompson Clark," he said, "Charleston Homicide." South Carolina was a long way from here, but he didn't seem to care he was outside his jurisdiction when he looked around as though he had every right to be present. "I understand Sunny Thicker was found dead." He finally met Allie's gaze with his own. "How can I help?"

# CHAPTER EIGHT

I needn't have worried, Allie's immediate reaction putting the detective in his place.

"Chief Crown," she said, making no effort whatsoever to accommodate past that pointed intro. "You knew the victim, detective?"

His expression flashed from dominating confidence to a flicker of irritation at her attitude. "I'm here on vacation, chief," he said, stressing that word like it didn't matter to him who she was or what she thought she knew.

"How nice for you," she said, droll as all get out, forcing me to cover the grin that made its way to my lips behind one hand. "Enjoying the sunshine, are you? Oh, you didn't answer my question." She paused then, same flat tone, same empty expression, unimpressed and cold. "Detective."

I guess it finally sank in he wasn't dealing with some local bumpkin because his demeanor shifted in response to at least a bit more respectful.

"Yes, I knew Sunny," he said, not exactly backing down from Allie, but giving her the attention she was due. "We're old friends."

"And you just happened to be visiting at the same time," my friend said.

He shrugged. "Look, I have ten years in homicide. I'm offering my help, chief. Take it or leave it."

Allie never missed a beat. "Leave it," she said, waving for one of her officers to join them. Thompson Clark's immediate rebellion died when my friend turned from him. "Please escort the detective to the office. We'll be having a more thorough conversation shortly."

He left with the uniform, scowling back over his shoulder at Allie who eye-rolled at me without shifting her body position, tossing her head once he was out of sight.

"Wait until he finds out you're former LA homicide," I grinned.

"Idiot," she snarled. "Arrogant ass, misogynistic jerk." Allie rarely swore, a fun fact I teased her about sometimes. The string of words she'd just used? Amounted to her cussing him up one side and down the other. "Maybe I should let him in on the investigation so I can keep an eye on him."

"I'd apologize," Carter said with a shrug, "but *not all men* has a sour ring to it." He finished stripping off his overalls as he went on. "As for the ligature, it has a distinct pattern that's still forming. I'll know more once the bruise finishes setting." Right. It could take up to twenty-four hours for perimortem marks to appear. "Seems like a thin strap of some kind, but with odd edges."

"Thanks, Carter." Allie nodded to him while he saluted both of us with one big hand before turning and going after the body. I watched him go, finally distracted from my work worries as one of the officers delivered a handbag to the chief.

"You know," she said, "you really need to ask him out already."

The squeaking giggle that escaped me had me shaking my head. I may have been a grown-assed woman with a business to run, but something about him made me devolve into an introverted teenager with just a look. Allie didn't pressure me further, so I finally sighed and turned back as she rifled through the gorgeous chocolate brown bag with gloved hands, the leather corner embroidered with a $ in gold to match the chain strap. Well, one strap. The other was missing, obviously torn free from the damage done to the leather on the other side.

"No wallet or phone," she said, handing it back to her officer who bagged it. "Could be robbery." She didn't sound convinced.

"Or made to look like it." I'd been at enough crime scenes of my own to know murderers thought themselves clever in the panic after the fact by trying to shift focus from themselves to a random mugging. Sadly, it worked often enough I'd been grateful to leave a job that only led to convictions a little over half the time.

Allie just nodded. "Why did she come back here?" I had the same question on my mind, didn't like any of the varying implications my brain led me to, if only because my bar was at the center of what was very likely a murder investigation, Carter's unwillingness to admit it or not.

"I know this is the last thing you want me to ask…" I didn't have to finish.

My friend waved one hand in the air between us with a wry grin. "Open Low Key," she said, "but we have to finish here before the bar is cleared, okay?"

I had that much, at least. "Thanks, Al."

While I know they weren't trying to be slow, and that Allie's goal was to solve the crime while being thorough, it was after 3PM before she finally cleared me to open Off Key's shutters and welcome guests. Considering it was a Friday night, I fretted the entire time, doing my best to stay out of her way so she wouldn't see me pacing, muttering and glaring at the officers and single forensics tech gathering what evidence they could while sifting through sand—dear God, *sand*—around the bar (do you know how much sand is on a beach? That's how much they searched).

I was in a bit of a froth, I admit it, by the time she texted me her go-ahead, so I was glad she didn't try to tell me in person. Likely, she was well aware of my mood and kept her distance on purpose. I adored her, called her a good friend, but there were some things that we both knew didn't mix well.

My financial security and murder investigations were on that list.

I let Pika deal with the grumbling locals, surprised when she showed for her shift, though when I tried to send her off to help Carter, she shrugged.

"I did my job," she said. "Now I'm here for this one." No emotion flashed, only cool logic. I wasn't about to argue with her because, quite frankly, I really needed her tonight. That meant her unruffled and uncaring attitude was all that was needed to silence nosy questioners with cold beers and a total lack of empathy from her adorably empty expression. It occurred to me I still hadn't seen Jasper and was now officially a horrible friend for putting money ahead of his unknown welfare and location when a woman sat down at the corner of the bar. A woman I'd seen last night, fighting with the victim, not to mention leaving the gas station with Sunny's ex-husband.

Chrissy Younger wasn't alone this time, either. Thing was, Melrose Lewis was nowhere in sight. Instead, her companion tucked in next to her, head down, in the shade of the far corner of the bar, Homicide Detective Thompson Clark close enough to her they had to be familiar with one another.

"Tequila sunrise," Chrissy said, barely looking at me, while Thompson ignored me completely. Which gave me a reason to stand close enough to them to eavesdrop, didn't it, when the homicide detective hissed something that had my ears perking.

"I'm listening," he said. "Tell me about the scam."

# CHAPTER NINE

Whether Thompson missed the fact I'd been standing next to Allie earlier or just wrote me off as a bartender I had no idea, but regardless I now had a front-row stand to the conversation that had me more than a little intrigued.

"I'm tired of the lies." Chrissy sipped the layered drink I slid to her across the bar, pink lip gloss leaving a ring on the end of her straw while Thompson ignored the beer I set in front of him. With Pika on the other end, I had more than enough reason to remain in my spot, nodding to the next person asking for a drink while staying in earshot of the unfolding conversation. "Their deceit. It's been going on too long. It was bound to all come out. And now Sunny is dead…" she hiccupped a soft sound before taking another delicate drink, big, blue eyes blinking at the homicide detective, fake lashes fluttering under artfully created brows, her soft, reddish curls framing her face in a style meant for someone Pika's age. "I didn't mean to fall in love with him, you have to believe me." Thompson didn't comment as she rambled on, one hand resting on his forearm he used to prop himself up on the bar. "I wish I'd never agreed to any of it. Sunny made it sound so easy, though, you know?"

Thompson's steady attention distracted both of them, I guess, and me along with them, because we were all surprised when Melrose Lewis stomped his way into their private conversation. The fact I'd banned him seemed irrelevant, something I'd be more than happy to deal with in short order. Just as soon as I took care of the customers in front of me. Which meant I lost track of them for about twenty seconds, grinding my teeth against the need to open a new bottle of chardonnay that meant a trip to the wine cooler before I could regain my place and serve the six-ounce glass to my next customer. Fortunately, I didn't think I missed much, because Melrose was talking, and it sounded like he hadn't stopped since he landed.

"—everything, Chrissy," he was saying, threat in his tone, in the way he loomed over her, something Thompson did nothing to defend her against while she cowed away from the furious man. "I know you have evidence that Sunny screwed me over on the divorce. I want it, and I'm not taking your excuses any longer."

The woman's face had crumpled, and I had a feeling from her hurt and tearful expression I now knew who the "he" was she'd referred to and that Melrose didn't return her feelings. While I'd seen them together last night, I hadn't jumped to the conclusion they were a couple. Clearly, Chrissy thought so or had until now. The fact she had a thing for the victim's ex-husband had me wanting to ask a ton of questions that were none of my business.

Oh, a thing about me and minding my own? I sucked at it.

"Back off, Mr. Lewis." The detective's drawling disregard for the other man's obvious anger had Melrose turning his attention away from the quivering woman and focusing it on Thompson.

"What are you doing here, Clark?" So, they knew one another, did they? Since Thompson claimed he'd known Sunny, was there a connection I was missing? Had to be. But did it have anything to do with why someone would want her killed?

Okay, just to set something straight. I wasn't eavesdropping for my own good, I swear. People talked openly around bartenders all the time, forgot we were even people, treated us like we were stupid, even. Honestly, that suited me just fine. Because if they gave me something I could take to Allie, it would mean solving the crime quicker and the kerfuffle dying down faster instead of being drawn out or—giant sigh—never getting resolved.

I was all for the former.

Turned out I didn't have to have my friend's back after all. In fact, she covered her own very well, striding with that casual lope of hers around the crowd and to the three in heated conversation at the end of the bar.

"Mr. Lewis." She offered a soft kind of smile that meant she wasn't in the mood for games herself. "I've been looking for you." I almost opened my mouth to ask her to get him out of my place, to enforce my ban, but decided to err on the side of letting her handle things. I had a feeling he wasn't going to be hanging around much longer anyway.

"Chief Crown." Thompson nodded to her. "Finally."

She didn't spare him even a moment's notice. "I asked you to meet me at my office, Mr. Lewis. I don't like having to chase people down."

He shrugged his narrow shoulders like she'd leave him alone if he could just get the angle right. "I have nothing to say without a lawyer."

"That's fine with me," she said, gesturing for him to precede her. "You can just wait for said lawyer's arrival in my company."

Melrose looked like he wanted to argue, but Thompson's dark chuckle had him frowning deeply.

"How about I escort you?" He stood, leaving Chrissy to look back and forth between them. "That all right with you, Chief Crown?" His choice of deferral all of a sudden had me wondering if he'd done a background check on her after all, or if she'd simply put him in his place when they'd chatted at her office.

"Fine with me." She spun and marched off, the two men following, the trembling and now weeping woman at the bar finishing her drink in three long swallows, bypassing the straw. I was already making her another without waiting for her to order and set it down in front of her before the glass hit the counter with a thud.

She took it without hesitation, taking another long drink, patting at her eyes with the cocktail napkin I slid her way.

"Thank you," she said.

"Need anything else?" I wanted to probe for

more, but she gave up the goods without me having to say another word.

"I'm a horrible friend," she burst into tears. "I blew it and now I'm out and I can't stand it."

Out. What did that mean?

Apparently, she'd been looking for someone to spill to, because she hunkered down and carried on while I let Pika deal with our customers and gave Chrissy my attention. "I followed the plan like everyone else," she wailed, one hand reaching out to grasp mine, fingernails digging into my wrist, hot palm sweaty and slippery on my skin. I let her hang on for a moment before pulling away, though Chrissy didn't seem to notice, waving the napkin at her face where moisture had risen to the surface. The faintly floral scent of her perfume reached me as she fanned herself while she carried on her confession. "Why did I get Melrose, of all people? I should have told them I wanted someone else, anyone else. I should have told Sunny how I felt about him. But I thought I'd be okay. I really did."

Now, I might have been utterly confused, but I did my best not to show it, offering up the classic bartender nod of genuine understanding and concern while pouring her another drink. She finished her second sunrise and reached for the third, two shots of tequila already reaching her bloodstream as she sipped the third and cleared her throat.

"I swear, I didn't go back to him until after the divorce." Wait, what did that mean? "I tried to stay away, but I love him." She stared down into her drink, expression a mix of horror and desire. "She couldn't fault me for that. But she did, after the fact." Chrissy met my eyes then, her pale blue ones earnest and begging for forgiveness. "I didn't mean to tell him what we'd done. I betrayed them and I'm sorry, but I couldn't lie to Melrose any longer."

It was a tribute to my bartender game I didn't grab her by the shoulders and shake her while demanding to know what the heck she was talking about. Thing was, my instincts she'd be spilling the pertinent details any second now panned out, so I didn't have to show her just how frustrating it was not to just blurt the question and ask.

"It's all going to come out now that Sunny's dead," Chrissy said at barely above a whisper, lower lip trembling, forcing me to lean in to catch her words. "They already hate me, but when their husbands find out…" She sighed deeply, shoulders sagging as she gave in to the tequila and her guilt and shrugged a delicate motion that had her strawberry waves shuddering. "Our pact fell apart and it's my fault. But they'll pay, too, when their ex-husbands find out what we did. How we set them up with prenups to make sure when each of us lured one of them they'd lose everything."

I gaped as loops of logic coalesced into understanding. "You cheated with one another's husbands to trigger your prenups?"

Chrissy shook her head with grim guilt. "We were supposed to hire, all cash, no trail. No trace we were involved. And it worked, too," she said. "Sunny's brilliant plan to ensure the sisterhood came out ahead actually worked." She'd fallen into dazed surprise. "And we would have gotten away with it. Until I ruined everything."

# CHAPTER TEN

Wow, just… holy heck. I felt like a drink myself after that little reveal, but Chrissy wasn't done.

"I'm happy I'm out," she said then, saluting me with her drink. "That the truth is out. I can't live with it anymore." Chrissy set her glass down without sipping this time, settling into a calm that felt more like acceptance after grief than actually taking responsibility for what she did. "You know what's the worst? Melrose dumped me after I told him. And my ex? He's married again already." She coughed a laugh. "They're pregnant." That seemed to break her all over again, face twisting into sorrow so deep I almost took the drink from her.

But Chrissy pulled herself together, sitting back, dabbing at her tears with the fresh napkin I handed her. "I'm free," she whispered then, smiled a little. "I should be grateful, right?"

Regardless of the bartender code? I couldn't think of a single thing to say. I was too busy considering the fact that Sunny's ex-husband had an excellent motive for murder.

My phone vibrated in my pocket, and I almost ignored it. I usually turned it off and only checked at break times. But considering it could have been Allie, I slipped it out for a quick look and immediately answered when I realized it was the friend I'd worried about on and off since last night.

"Jasper," I gasped his name, forgetting Chrissy in the moment. "Are you okay?"

"I'm at the chief's office," he said, voice low and vibrating with emotion. "Can you come? I think she's going to arrest me for murder."

Like *hell* she was. "On my way." I turned back to find Chrissy had left, her third empty drink and a wad of cash left behind. No worries, I'd pursue her issues later. Meanwhile, I had a friend to rescue from another friend.

Pika eye-rolled when I brought Ox in to fill my position, the pair comical enough behind the bar together it would have been hilarious if I'd been in a different frame of mind. As it was, I drove a little too fast the five minutes it took me to peel out of the Low Key parking lot and pull up outside the Canary Key police station, slamming my door and trotting up the stairs to the glass entry with all kinds of persuasive words in my head to convince Allie to let Jasper go. Including and not exclusive to the fact the victim's ex-husband was an excellent suspect.

Brit Clairmont waved me through, the office receptionist not even bothering to ask me what was up. I hurried through the bullpen and to Allie's office at the back, the recently renovated and bright interior of the station a distinct change from the ones I was used to in Manhattan, the almost tropical feel of the yellow painted walls and cheerfully modern décor giving the station a cartoon cop sense of esthetic I knew irritated the chief with its happy-go-lucky design. Not that I was paying attention as I strode to Allie's door and let myself in without knocking.

To find Jasper sitting in front of her desk, the chief herself perched on the edge with her arms crossed and an eyebrow raising at the sight of me charging in, ready to rescue our mutual friend.

Allie didn't comment on my presence, though my leaving the bar at the height of dinner hour on Friday was an oddity of its own. Instead, she nodded to Jasper. "Go on."

He looked my way with a rueful expression, handsome face apologetic. "Like I was saying," he said, no longer frantic, apparently, or being arrested, either. I scowled as adrenaline relinquished its hold on me. "I never met her before last night. And once her friend came and got her, I went home. That's it."

I was going to kill him. Not only was he alive and well and unharmed, he'd dragged me down here for nothing. "I saw you two leave her hotel last night." I hadn't meant to sound so accusatory, but Jasper reminded me a lot of Gray, too much. The kid brother protective complex I carried around had transferred to him, and I had no illusions otherwise. "I've been messaging you all day." Okay, so I'd started messaging him after Allie left, after the body was taken away, and definitely after worrying about my bottom line. And in between work jags. But hey, I *had* messaged him.

He tossed his hands with an adorable grimacing smile that I was sure worked on women who were attracted to him and didn't see him as a friend who needed his head examined.

"My phone died," he said by way of explanation to both of us. "I was sleeping last night off when your officer showed up at the cottage." He lived in an adorable one-bedroom he'd inherited from his grandmother that still had the old lady esthetic going on. That mixed with hardcore bachelor meant I was surprised someone like Sunny hadn't run screaming.

Wait, maybe she had and that's why her friends came to get her. But if that was the case, why mention Jasper at all?

"For the second time today," Allie said. "Jimmy said he knocked both times, Jasper." All droll again. This was going to end well. I wasn't the only one annoyed with the perpetual teenager.

"Sorry, I swear," he said. "I didn't even know Sunny, you know." He flinched. "Is she really dead?"

Allie sighed and circled her desk to sit heavily, shaking her head at him. "You're useless," she snapped. "Just go home, Jasper."

He stood slowly, hesitant, but grinned at her, that boyish charm surfacing like it always did. "If I think of anything else, I'll tell you." He winked then. "I am a trained PI, remember? I could help if you want? I do know the ladies pretty well."

"Jasper," Allie snarled. "Out."

While he might not have been astute about many things, Jasper Dunlop knew when to get when the getting was good. I watched him go, still on the fence between hugging him and throttling him over this ridiculous visit that was quite obviously unnecessary and unwelcome. I turned back to Allie whose sour expression told me as much, which had me reaching for a good reason for being here and delivering, thank goodness, with what I'd heard from Chrissy.

Allie's attention shifted almost immediately from irritated to interested as she took in the sisterhood pact with a growing frown. "Every time I think I've heard it all," she said.

"Right?" I hesitated to break the moment I'd managed to save with a question but failed utterly. "Sounds like Melrose might be your guy."

She didn't argue, maybe partially because of our history and partially because of my training. At least I knew my way around a crime scene. Jasper's little PI comment—and his joyful exploration of multiple jobs that required more effort than he was willing to commit to—wasn't helping matters. Though, I realized a moment later as she let out an uncharacteristic, "Crap!" I wasn't the focus of her attention. "I forgot to ask him which friend came to get Sunny at his place. Argh, that man makes me mental."

That made both of us. Because it wasn't like Allie to forget details, nor me to leave my bar for any reason. Except, it turned out when it came to the adorably frustrating friend we had in common.

None of which was important as Carter Wilson poked his head around Allie's door and met my gaze with a warm smile.

"Hope I'm not interrupting," he said.

Oh, he was, and welcome, at that. Saved by the hot doc, my favorite.

## CHAPTER ELEVEN

Allie waved him inside while I did my best to appear unobtrusive, Carter still casually dressed in shorts and a t-shirt. I'd seen him in a suit once and caught myself drooling, not that he was any less gorgeous looking like he should be surfing instead of delivering information on a murder.

"I've confirmed TOD," he said, handing Allie a file, the scent of fresh air and some low-key sandalwood variant wafting to me, subtle enough I found myself leaning closer to catch the full bouquet of it and only managing to stop before I got close enough to fall into him. Burying my face in his shirt to take a nice, long sniff wasn't going to earn me points with the chief or endear me to Carter, so I held back as best I could, keeping my expression as neutral as possible.

Yeah, I wasn't fooling anyone, was I?

"2AM," Allie said, studying the paperwork he'd given her. She looked up, met my eyes. "You said you saw the vic and Jasper leaving the hotel at what time?"

Right, a chance to be all official and such. Allie had no idea the lifeline she'd thrown me.

"About one-thirty," I said. "Maybe a little after." It had taken me twenty minutes to cash out and close up, deposit the day's receipts and catch Jasper kissing Sunny, so my guess was close enough.

"Two is a solid time?" Allie turned to Carter who nodded.

"Even accounting for the warm evening." He didn't exactly chide her, but it was obvious he was confident. The fact he accepted her need for reassurance without taking it as an attack on his competence was just another lovely thing about him. "There was no evidence of any kind of tampering with the body after the fact, so her liver temp is accurate based on blood alcohol level and ambient temperature."

Allie grunted as she freed a photograph he'd added in the file, turning it toward him and giving me a view at the same time. It was pretty obvious the bruise was COD, the flesh cut deeply over the windpipe, crushing the cartilage that formed the trachea. No way she'd have survived that without immediate attention once her airway collapsed. Whoever did this to her had some solid strength behind the effort. I'd seen strangulations that ended in death just from blood flow being interrupted, but this? This was next-level aggression. "Any ideas what caused it?"

I had one with a jolt of surprise as he nodded.

"A decent width of chain," he said as I spoke over him.

"Purse strap." We exchanged a startled look before I turned back to Allie. "Sunny's purse strap. It's chain."

She stared at me with narrowed eyes, but not out of anger, I knew that much. I could see her brain churning behind her gaze as she set the photo aside. "I'll have forensics check it for foreign DNA. Good job, Carter. Nice catch, Becks." That was Allie, giving credit where it was due, though I had no doubt she'd made the same leap herself.

With the chief hitting the phone and our presence no longer required, I left when Carter did, struggling against the awkward feeling I seemed to settle into when in his presence, hands tucking into my back pockets, reaching for the confident forty-year-old woman I'd grown into and begging her not to let me down as he held the door for me and waited for me to exit ahead of him. It wasn't until we reached our respective vehicles—his truck parked next to my Jeep—that I paused and turned to smile up at him.

Determined not to make a fool of myself.

"I know you're busy," Carter said before I could speak first, "but if you find the time, I'd love to get a coffee." He hesitated while my brain emptied itself out onto the sidewalk and I gaped at him in stunned silence. "Or something?"

Dear. God. *What*. Babble.

I must have said yes amid my freakish loss of conscious ability to speak of my own recognizance because Carter smiled at me a moment later.

"Great," he said. "I'm in town for the week, taking some time off." He shrugged his broad shoulders. "At least, I meant to." That made him laugh and I laughed too, I think, while he went on. "I'll call you?"

And then he was gone, driving off while I came to on the sidewalk, having no idea what just happened except that I somehow managed not to scare him away.

A *date*. I had a *date* with *Carter Wilson*.

To say I floated the whole way back to Off Key would be an understatement. I probably shouldn't have been driving, though I somehow found myself behind the bar, beaming at everyone, pouring drinks and laughing and feeling about as high as if I'd had two shots of my own offerings before coming back to work.

I barely noticed when Bruno arrived, or when Pika shot me weird looks, or that Jasper wandered in a short time later, setting up for the evening's 80s themed dance party. In fact, it wasn't until I'd cleared my section of the bar, music rising from the speakers where DJ Dun-It (I know, cheesy, but that was Jasper) bopped to the tunes he pumped out that my mood altered.

Suddenly and with a sharp intake of breath. Because the sight of the creepy Latino guy in the blue work clothes? The one from the night before, the one who'd been watching Sunny and Jasper kiss outside the hotel and then lurked here this morning after Allie arrived? Drove the breath from my lungs when I caught sight of him staring right at Jasper like my friend was his next target.

Next? You better believe I jumped to a conclusion. That had me leaving the bar so fast Bruno barked at me, racing around the edge of the dancefloor and confronting the man.

Who took one look at my charging approach and ran.

Now, chasing a possible murder suspect wasn't

the brightest, I get that. But I had my dad's instincts and a head of steam, and I'd been riding high since Carter's suggestion we have coffee or something. All that excess of hormonal surging had clearly altered my brain chemistry enough to shift me out of caution and into confrontation. Which meant, as the man in the navy-blue work pants and shirt who'd caught my attention for the third time tried to run across the sand in his heavy boots, my nimble sneakers were much faster.

He did make it around the palm trees at the edge of my property line before I tackled him, so at least my customers didn't see me hurtle myself in ungainly aggression at the stranger. The full force of my weight carried him to the ground, his grunt of surprise turning to a cry of anger as I sprang to my feet, bouncing on my toes, ready to go to battle.

Stupid, yes. When he stood, I realized he was bigger than me by at least half a foot and heavier by a lot. Not that I wasn't capable of defending myself, but I may have gone a bit far, in retrospect. Though, when Ox came charging around the corner a moment later, my nervousness I'd done something epically ridiculous I'd learn to regret died in the face of reinforcement.

Sizeable reinforcement. If the stranger had intended to fight back, he'd given up that play at the sight of my looming staff member, his dark eyes now fixed on Ox's remarkably bulky self while I reached for my phone.

"Tell me why I shouldn't call Chief Crown," I snarled. "And have you arrested for murder." Oh, dear. That was a leap, I knew it. He'd done what? Watched two people kiss? Checked out a crime scene along with a bunch of other gawkers? Glared at my friend?

Except there was enough guilt in his face, in the hunched way he seemed to try to protect himself from my gaze, I knew I'd trusted my instincts for the right reasons.

"Ms. Hogan," he said, surprising me that he knew my name, holding up both hands while I tried to place him. I'd thought I'd recognized him last night but from where? "I'm Valentine Ortega. I work maintenance at the golf course. I didn't kill anyone." He sighed, dropping his hands. "But I'm glad she's dead." He gestured toward the bar past the trees, the sound of music almost drowning him out. "Sunny Thicker was the prosecutor who sent me to prison after falsifying evidence that got me convicted of a crime I didn't commit."

## CHAPTER TWELVE

I honestly didn't know what to say to that and didn't interfere when Ox, his squished nose wrinkling when he squinted in sympathy, bent to assist Valentine to his feet. As my bouncer brushed sand from the man's work clothes, I attempted to process what he'd said, but didn't ask any questions.

Turned out questions weren't necessary.

"I got out last year," Valentine said, faint hint of a Spanish accent sounding more Americanized than not, long, lean face drawn out in regret and anger, dark eyes damp under his thick, black brows and the heavy fall of his overhang of bangs. "I just wanted to get past it, move on. So, I left Charleston and moved here, to Canary Key." I did recognize him now, embarrassed by my lack of attention and that I'd jumped to a conclusion I maybe shouldn't have. Biased or racist, Becks? I didn't want to think I was either, but I knew better. Both crept in no matter my intentions, I was sure of it. The fact I golfed once a week since moving here and now remembered encountering Valentine multiple times over those months had me blushing and nodding for him to go on.

Not that he needed encouragement. Maybe having someone stand there and listen to him made him open up more than he might have normally, but whatever the reason, Valentine spilled the tea on his situation without me prompting past that head bob of understanding.

"Mr. Halston was nice to give an ex-con a job." Craig Halston owned and ran the local eighteen-hole course. Hardly an award-winning layout, but it served its purpose. "I thought I could leave it all behind me." Valentine wiped at his trembling lips, thin mustache bristling against his rough hand. "Then *she* shows up." Sunny, right. His dark eyes met mine, anger rising to supersede sad desperation. "You know what was the worst part?" Ox shook his head right along with me, the pair of us intent on Valentine's story. "She didn't even recognize me."

My bouncer grunted in sympathy, big hand patting Valentine's shoulder while I felt even guiltier than ever I'd run this poor man down. Except, of course, he had a motive for murder, didn't he? If what he'd said was true?

"I know what you're thinking," he gushed immediately while Ox shot me a chastising look that had me glaring back in defense. "I swear, I didn't kill her. I just wanted her to admit she'd set me up." Valentine tossed his hands, sighed deeply, staring down at the toes of his heavy work boots. "I didn't even need her to say it officially. I just wanted her to apologize to me. So, I confronted her." He rubbed at both arms with his big hands.

Wait, he did what? "Do not tell me another word," I snapped. Spun on Ox and gestured for him to go immediately. My employee almost didn't, clear resistance on his face while Valentine stared at me in surprise. I grasped the ex-con— innocent or not—by one arm and dragged him toward the parking lot and my Jeep while Ox finally did as he was told, though I noted he checked in on us over one big shoulder as I herded Valentine to my vehicle and pointed for him to climb inside.

He did, though his expression had turned to concern. "Where are we going?"

Good thing I always kept my keys with me. I fired up the engine and peeled out into the early evening under the cold, white streetlights, passing traffic at a rate that would have gotten me pulled over if one of Allie's officers spotted me. Instead, I made a second trip to the chief's office in less time than the first had. "You're going to tell Allie Crown everything," I said, "so there are no more mistakes, Valentine." Yes, I know. He could have killed Sunny. Just because he said he didn't, that wasn't any reason to believe him. And yet, I did. Not only believed but wanted to make up for the horrible assumptions and conclusion jumps I'd made. Which meant doing what I could to ensure he got a fair shake.

Any other cop? I'd worry. But Allie wouldn't treat him like I had, I was sure of that.

He cringed in the front seat, pale light overhead casting his face in shadows as I parked at the office's front door. When I turned to him, however, he didn't argue or try to fight me when I pointed at the glass entry.

"You need to get ahead of this," I said. "Trust me, Valentine. There will be people who think you did kill Sunny because of the story you told me. Allie Crown isn't one of them."

He looked back and forth between me and the office, then nodded. "I know," he said, voice small but firm. "I wanted to talk to the chief, but I didn't know how to do it without it looking like it looked to you." I winced at that, but fair enough.

"I'm coming in with you," I said. Overboard on the protective department? Maybe, but guilt and a sense of regret mingled with my ingrained habit of defending the defenseless to the point I was determined to be his advocate no matter what.

Allie hadn't left her office yet and, to her credit, sat and listened while Valentine filled her in on everything. How Sunny Thicker was an assistant prosecutor early in her career, how he'd been her last case and that the evidence against him was forged. The fact he had no proof definitely hung between the three of us, though Allie finally thanked him when Valentine wrapped up his side of the story with his one admission.

"I saw her at the bar last night," he said. "I followed her and Jasper Dunlop to the hotel." He glanced at me. "I saw you pull in. That's why I left." That meant he did see me. "I just wanted that apology. When I found her at the bar after her friends left, I confronted her. But she laughed at me." Tears rose in his earnest eyes, hands clasped tightly in his lap. "I swear, I walked away."

"Her friends?" Allie leaned in at that. "You saw her friends at the bar? After it closed?"

He nodded immediately. "I didn't hear what

they were saying, but they were all very upset. Then they left." He shrugged a little.

Allie stood, heading for me, nodding to Valentine. "I have a few more questions," she said to him before guiding me firmly out of her office and closing the door on him. Her steady gaze held mine the whole time while I tried not to read anything into her calm expression. "Do I need to get you a badge, Becks?"

I laughed, a short, barking sound of surprise that made her grin. "No thanks," I said.

"Okay then," she winked. "How about you leave the police work to the ones who *do* have badges if that's the case?" Allie went back into her office without another word while I exhaled a long, slow breath. I'd hit the end of her patience rope, then.

Good to know she was human and had one.

As for me? I headed back to work. Where I belonged.

# CHAPTER THIRTEEN

When I returned, I found Jasper taking a break from his DJ gig, sparkling behind the bar, giving Pika a necessary helping hand. It was clear from Ox's forlorn expression the playboy hadn't given my employee an opportunity to join his love interest again. Instead, cheerful as ever, my friend's bout with the law apparently unable to phase his confidence or the charisma, had sold enough drinks to make up for the fact he hadn't told me he was okay.

He quickly gave way to me when I slipped in beside him, returning to spinning tunes. And while he was good at everything he did, his heart wasn't into slinging drinks, not if he couldn't be the center of attention.

That role fell entirely to Pika. She shot me a blank look—her favorite from someone who gleefully acted like the perfect automaton and prided herself on it—when I shook my head at the lineup she dealt with as calmly as if they didn't exist.

That girl earned her tips by being mean and cold and it cracked me up.

Not that it kept me from joining in the fun. Now that I'd tidied up the Valentine mess, I could get back to what I loved. Friday evening meant throwing myself gleefully into tossing bottles and taking cash for the privilege.

I guess I shouldn't have been surprised that the three friends showed up, the women who didn't appear to be so much grieving as they were regretful ordering a solid round of tequila shots, staying at the bar to toss them back after clinking in salute. They'd dressed down tonight, no more slinky dresses or high heels in evidence, opting for shorts and shells though still above-average compared to the bulk of my guests.

"To Sunny," Nina said.

"Sunny," Hannah and Latoya echoed, the three wincing as the strong spirit made its way down their throats. Limes and salt followed, a second round already poured to drown their sorrows in. I had a brief lull moment, long enough to offer a third when the second vanished.

"This one's on me," I said. Not that I handed out free booze on the regular, but their friend had died at my place and whether that was my fault or not, I still felt a little guilty about it.

Their soft cheer of thanks ended with another toss, swallow, lick and bite. Hannah set her purse on the bar with a thud, reaching into it for a wad of cash, while I stared in surprise, surveying the other three a moment.

"You all have the same bag." They did, identical. Well, crap, down to the chain straps and all. But wait. "Yours is a yin yang?" Hannah nodded, Nina, holding hers up, showing off an embroidered star, while Latoya's had that medical symbol I could never remember the name of.

A caduceus. Yeah, that was it.

"Sunny's idea," Nina said, burping delicately, already flushed from the tequila hitting her system.

"She always had big ideas." Latoya's rapid descent into glum and grim had the other two nodding in their own despair.

"Even Chrissy?" Maybe I shouldn't have brought up their ex-friend, but they all bobbed nods as Hannah handed over the cash for their shots. My offer of another round was waved off, though they each ordered a cocktail while Hannah answered.

"Even Chrissy. The traitor." They were taking up valuable real estate at the bar, the line behind them growing, but there was no polite way to ask them to move along. And besides, my moment of *ah-ha!* had turned from solving Sunny's murder to adding these three—along with their former friend—to the list of suspects.

Five purses with matching chain straps that might or might not have been the murder weapon. Awesome. I'd tell Allie the second I had time, but it wasn't a slam dunk I was going to hand her, so I actually considered minding my own business.

The girls didn't seem to mind my prodding, however, tequila's lovely tongue loosening properties usually encouraging happiness, but only serving to make the three of them chatty and catty.

"We should never have listened to her." Who, Chrissy? Though when Latoya leaned into Hannah, sipping the daiquiri I'd made her while I slid a beer around her to the customer behind her with a wave and apologetic grin, I realized the gorgeous doctor referred to the victim. "Why did we listen to Sunny?"

"Now everyone's going to know." Nina squinted at me, wobbling slightly, the tequila clearly hitting her. For all I knew, the three had been drinking prior to arrival and this was just the next level. Or the entrepreneur couldn't hold her alcohol. Either way, she seemed on the brink of intoxication already. "*You* know, right?" I didn't get to answer and had no idea what the question was. Until a lightbulb came on at her next words. "We're all going to get sued. My ex will take me for everything."

Ah. They knew the gig was up and the scam revealed. Not that I felt bad for them, honestly, but a good bartender knows when to commiserate and when to cut someone off and I was in the mood to make as much money from them as possible without putting them in danger.

Served them right.

"Chrissy told that cop everything." Hannah's whining tone made them all wince.

"Why did we listen?" Latoya slapped one hand on the bar, making the young woman behind her jump as she took possession of the glass of wine I'd poured her. I quickly lined up three more tequila shots, sliding them off to one side, the lure of the glasses tugging on the trio of friends like a magnet and moving them out of my serving lane. That way, I got to monitor them and keep business rolling at the same time.

"Some friend," I muttered. Hey, I wasn't above prodding drunk women with terrible life decisions behind them for information if I could help my friend put a murderer away.

"Right?" Nina swallowed her shot, not bothering with salt or lime this time. "Maybe it's a good thing Sunny's dead. Now everything's out in the open and we can just stop pretending." Didn't sound like she really thought that was for the best.

I glanced up as Pika served Thompson Clark a beer before the homicide detective spun and walked away, turning to stare at the women from a small table on the edge of the sand. And had a thought.

"You're all from Charleston, right?" I paused to refill their tequila again while they nodded like a trio of birds at a feeder. "You guys know anything about Thompson Clark?"

Nina snorted. "That cop Sunny was into?" Oh, *was* she now? "Yeah, he's been hanging around for years."

"Thought Sunny was in love with him." Latoya snorted a laugh while Hannah's cruel giggle joined in.

"Melrose even tried to prove they had an affair once upon a time," the therapist said, one small hand clutching her purse while the other cradled the tequila shot. "Like that got him anywhere."

Speak of the devil's ex-husband, I noted Melrose Lewis as he passed the bar, and kept an eye on him when he stopped at the sight of

Thompson Clark. What was I going to have to do to make sure he took my ban seriously? Sunny's ex spun and changed course, joining the line that would have Pika serve him, head down and avoiding the three women who never noticed his arrival.

"It's not like she had much to do with him anyway," Hannah said. "She wasn't in the prosecutor's office long."

"So, no scandal?" Whatever Thompson's reason for being here, I had a feeling it wasn't altruistic. I almost waved to Pika not to serve him and thought better of it as the women laughed in unison, Hannah's almost a donkey bray that ended in an indelicate snort.

"It was *Sunny*," Nina said, leaning into the bar with a giant smile. "There was *always* a scandal."

"She knew where the money was," Latoya said, setting her shot glass down with a thud. "The minute she could, she jumped into family law." One of her big, dark eyes winked at me. "That's why I chose plastics." She nodded at Hannah who hiccupped and sagged into the bar, tiny body wavering. "Why Hannah here chose therapy." Nina's dark eyes lifted to mine when Latoya finished. "And the star of the show went into business for herself."

Nina saluted me with her final shot.

"And Chrissy?" I needed to leave this alone. I was busy and they were a distraction. But I was honestly curious and since most of the orders coming in barely required attention—beers and wine and more beers—I could split my focus, even if it meant lower tips.

The three women snorted, but it was Nina who answered.

"Accountant," she eye-rolled while the women laughed. "At least she followed that part of Sunny's strategy to the core."

"High-paying job of power," Latoya nodded.

"Attract a wealthy husband," Hannah said.

"And take him for everything." Nina sighed. "Where did we go wrong?"

Um. Did they really want an answer to that question? Like, an answer from a normal and reasonably well-adjusted person?

Apparently not.

"We trusted Sunny," Latoya snarled suddenly.

"And Chrissy." Hannah almost moaned that.

I was surprised when Nina finally shook her head. "We did it to ourselves." Ah, so someone was willing to take responsibility, at least. She took her glass then, the rum and cola I'd made her on order sloshing over the side a little, drops smearing my bar and making me itch to wipe it clear. She nodded aggressively once, then shrugged. And wandered off, the ladies following, managing to snag a table near the dancefloor when the couple who'd occupied it chose that moment to leave.

As Police Chief Allie Crown decided to make another appearance.

## CHAPTER FOURTEEN

I meant to mind my own business, I really did. Except Allie showing up at my bar with two other officers kind of *was* my business, if you know what I mean. That meant I was out and dashing for the women's table before the chief made it, the two of us arriving at the same moment.

Allie's flat glance told me she acknowledged my presence but really hoped I'd keep my mouth shut. Considering she was about to make a scene? We'd see about that.

Friendship only went so far when cold hard cash was involved.

"Chief Crown." Latoya waved at her with a

wonky smile, Hannah's blinking stare empty of concern. Nina, however, seemed to register something was up and instantly reached across to her friends, shushing them before fixing Allie with a stare that told me the woman wasn't as drunk as she'd appeared. Or was just really good at regaining control of herself. Regardless of the truth, the other two listened when Nina spoke.

"You're not here for a drink," the woman said, glancing at me before turning back to Allie. "If you have more questions, you know our response." The other two nodded. "We're waiting for our lawyers, remember?"

Ah, so they'd lawyered up, had they? That made sense and was likely the reason for my friend's unhappily empty glare.

"I am aware," Allie said in a dull tone that cut through protests like a jackhammer. All three women paused, took note, despite their alcohol-influenced states. "I'm also aware of new evidence I'd like you to have a look at." She paused then, heavy and full of threat. "While we wait for your lawyers to show up." It was pretty clear to me Allie's patience with waiting was about on par with my own, and that was with knowing her as well as I did.

"And what evidence might that be?" Nina let out a soft burp that had to mean she was deeper into intoxication than she was willing to show. I'd give her credit for her collection in the face of opposition despite the tequila she'd downed. Working and owning restaurants must have given her a level of resilience I'd never developed. Partly because I never imbibed my own products.

Allie snapped her fingers at the two officers who moved forward while I winced and waved at some staring patrons, wanting to hurry the chief along. Thankfully, Jasper noticed my distressed state and spoke up over the crowd on the microphone he held, announcing his next music choice in his best DJ voice while Allie lowered hers.

"I now have proof the three of you were here around the time of Sunny's murder," she said. Turned and pointed back toward the parking lot. "While you were smart to avoid the cameras here at Low and Off Key, the convenience store across the street had a clear view of the beach." She'd already asked me for any footage I had. Of course, I'd tried to comply, only to be shocked to discover the last storm that rolled through damaged the cable connecting the bar's two cameras to the main system which meant, while they worked, nothing was being recorded.

What a way to find out.

All three women stared up at her, now silent

with a mix of sullen and anxious that had me wishing Allie would take this confrontation elsewhere.

"You three told me you hadn't seen her after she left with Jasper." Allie knew better. I was there when Valentine Ortega told her he'd seen them. "You lied to me, ladies. And now I have not only an eyewitness, I have video footage to prove it. So, like it or not, lawyers present or not, you're all coming back down to the office and will sit in a cell until your representation gets here."

Nina spluttered, Hannah bursting into tears while Latoya swayed in stunned anxiety. But they went the three of them, officers herding them out as I practically pushed them all along.

Just as Chrissy Younger showed up. She stopped in her tracks at the sight of the police surrounding her former friends. While Latoya stuck a trembling finger out at the gaping woman.

"She was there too," the doctor blurted, Nina's hissing for silence ignored this time. "And we left before she did. So, arrest *her*."

"I intend to talk to Ms. Younger as well," Allie said. "In fact, this is perfect timing since I have officers looking for you."

"But did you know she threatened Sunny?" That was Hannah, who'd managed to stop crying but whose trembling voice had filled with vitriol and venom fed more by fear, I guessed than anger. "You told her you wished she was dead."

Chrissy shook her head. "I didn't mean it. I was angry."

"So you say." Nina finally got her two cents in, hugging Hannah to her, the smaller woman leaning into the taller, stronger of the two while Latoya glared at their ex-friend like they'd just caught her red-handed. "Arrest her, Sheriff Crown."

Allie grit her teeth. "Chief," she snarled. Still, she nodded to Chrissy who backpedaled briefly, but almost fell as her platform sandal caught on the edge of the step, forcing her to stop or fall over. As she wobbled, her purse swung forward from her shoulder, the white and black checkered tote nothing like the one the other women carried. I guess her sense of sisterhood was in the trash with her matching bag.

Not that I would have blamed her for biffing it.

Her lack of balance gave Allie the time she needed to approach and include the now-shaking woman in the little circle of suspects she'd rounded up.

I hardly cared, to be honest. As long as she took them away from my place and stopped making a scene for the new customers walking past us and staring at the unfolding drama. Sure, I was happy to chat and listen in and find out what I could without making a fuss, but the chief didn't seem to have my level of circumspection.

Allie paused at the exit to the parking lot while I huffed in frustration at her attitude.

"I'm doing my job," she said.

"I'm trying to do mine," I shot back. "You could have been a bit more tactful."

"And you could have stayed out of it." We hadn't had a single rough word for one another since the moment we'd met six months ago. In fact, Allie had been the first person I'd encountered the day I'd signed the papers on the bar, coming for a drink to say so long to Conrad Metter and to welcome me to town. We'd been fast friends ever since. And while I hoped this situation wasn't going to put the kibosh to our relationship, no one put my livelihood at risk, especially after I'd given up everything to make this dream happen.

"Good luck with the investigation, Chief Crown." I turned my back on her and stomped back to the bar, waving at Jasper who carried on despite a concerned look aimed in my direction, my whole evening soured by the continuing controversy. And the sight of Thompson Clark and Melrose Lewis arguing not far from the corner of my bar?

About to get the pair of them bounced out of

my place and kicked off the key if I had anything to say about it. And since I did have something to say about it, it was time to call Ox and make sure this was the last time Melrose decided to ignore the fact I'd banned him. Except, as I reached for my phone to text the big bouncer to come do some biffing, the unwelcome guests in question split and went their separate ways, leaving me to glare after both of them in a huff that needed an outlet but wasn't going to get one.

It was a long night at the bar, and I only had my attitude to blame for my lack of tips.

# CHAPTER FIFTEEN

By the time I closed up for the night, I was still grouchy, though a nice scratch for Bruno and a snack from the restaurant fridge had me sorted out more or less. As I headed out, I noted the University of Florida van parked on the far corner of my lot and paused as the three scientists climbed out, lugging gear with them as they went.

The young woman waved to me with a cheerful, "Hey, Becks!" that had me going back inside and retrieving a few choice leftovers Marta Sanchez had prepared (mostly for Bruno, but some for me, too) before returning to the parking lot. The researchers had already crossed the sand to the little shack they'd erected three weeks ago, gaining permission to park in my lot at night when they told me why they were here on the key.

I scratched at the canvas flap, the bulk of the tent buried in sand to keep it camouflaged and handed over the paper containers with two burritos and a fresh dish of guacamole and chips to the beaming trio who immediately dove into the food.

"How's the turtle business?" The fact sea turtles were nesting here on this stretch of beach had me delighted and fascinated, though I hadn't checked in with the researchers in a few days.

"Awesome," Ricki Solet said, the Ph.D. candidate pushing her wire-rimmed glasses up her narrow nose, long, brown hair in a thick ponytail hanging over one shoulder, her t-shirt's cartoon turtle waving over the "Save Me!" written below. "We've tagged fourteen female loggerheads in the last week alone. And don't get me started on the two leatherbacks." She eye-rolled in delight while her male companions laughed. "Gorgeous girls. We're hoping they'll come nest, but it's a pretty active stretch of beach." She sounded so wistful.

"It'll happen," Jacob Piercer said, her co-researcher nodding to their professor, Dr. Noah Moshe. "Right, doc?"

"One of these years," he said, thick Israeli accent as exotic as his amber eyes and warm, brown skin. He winked at me, taking a big bite of burrito. "If only all key residents had your interest, Rebecca." He always insisted on my full first name and, while I didn't mind so much, it always sounded awesome coming from him.

Yes, I needed to date. I get it, okay? Lay off.

"I need a favor," I said. All three instantly nodded, pausing in their setup and chewing to wait for the ask. "Do you have any footage that covers Off Key from last night?" I was still kind of pissed at Allie, but she was my friend and I figured she hadn't asked because even I overlooked the small band of turtle hunters who hunkered here in a dirt-covered canvas hole in the sand. Or she'd thought of it and I'd wasted my time, but it was my time to waste.

Turned out it was the former. "As a matter of fact," Noah said, leaning over Ricki's shoulder and poking some keys on her laptop. I crouched, Bruno nudging his way inside and demanding pats from Jacob while I watched the video footage scroll on fast forward. It jumped from location to location several times before it came to a halt around 1AM early that morning.

I met Noah's eyes with a squint only to have him shrug.

"I am assuming you're asking can only be connected to the death of that woman," the biologist said. "I'm sorry I didn't think of it myself before now." He pointed at the screen. "The camera jumps locations once an hour, on a timer, but it may have caught something of use."

It had a pretty clear line of sight to Off Key, if far enough away to make details sketchy. Still, it could help Allie, so I hadn't wasted my time after all.

And then Sunny staggered into view and all thoughts of everything went out the window. The four of us watched, engrossed, as she sat at the bar alone, only to be confronted a moment later by her friends. She stood to face them, the three other women seemed angry, gesturing wildly around, one even pushing her. Sunny staggered back as Chrissy arrived from around the bar and confronted all four. The three friends left Sunny with their former sister who had her own shouting match—or so it looked—with the victim.

When Chrissy left, I exhaled deeply, especially when Valentine approached from the beach side, out of sight of the footage Allie already had access to. He'd told her as much, and so far his story panned out. After another argument—Sunny knew how to piss people off—I watched Valentine storm away. The feeling of relief he'd left her alive had me hoping there was something Allie could do for him. He'd been honest about his encounter with the victim and if he really was innocent of the crime she'd put him away for, he deserved to be compensated and cleared.

Sunny had another visitor a moment later as Melrose Lewis approached, sneaking through the beach like a thief as though creeping up on his ex-wife. This time the fight wasn't so explosive, though it appeared intense. Hard to tell, really, from that distance, though he, too, stormed away. I almost leaned back while Sunny sagged on the stool, arms crossing over the counter, head down. Except movement from the beach caught my attention as, to my surprise, Chrissy strode back toward the bar, purse swinging from her shoulder.

Her purse. The matching purse. At least, it looked that way to me. Sure, I could have been wrong. Like I said, it was a good hundred feet away, impossible to make out features, but I was sure I was right.

Before Chrissy could reach Sunny, however, the footage switched to an empty bit of sand and surf.

"That's everything, I'm afraid," Noah said, sounding breathlessly disappointed.

"And I thought watching turtles was exciting," Ricki said while Jacob grinned around a mouthful of food he shared with drooling Bruno.

"Can you make sure Allie gets a copy?" I was asking for them to share research footage without a warrant, but the biologist didn't flinch.

"Of course," he said. "I'll email it personally. Though I don't know if it will help." He skimmed the footage forward by two hours, the cycle of the camera's focus shifting back to the bar and the slumped form of Sunny, now very dead and still.

"I'm sure she'll appreciate it," I said. Took my leave with final pats for Bruno from the three, texting my chief friend what I'd found, and that the footage was on the way.

She messaged me almost immediately. *Got it*, she sent. *Thanks, Becks.*

So, we were still friends? I was surprised by the release of tension that simple text gave me and was in a much better mood as I climbed behind the wheel than I probably deserved to be. After all, I may have just seen a murderer just before she throttled her former friend with the straps of her sisterhood purse.

Yikes, relationships were complicated.

I had no idea how complicated. Until I pulled into my driveway to find Jasper sitting on my step, head in his hands. When he looked up and met my eyes, I groaned because I really didn't want to have to deal with his drama at 1:30AM.

Didn't get the choice though, did I?

"Becks," he groaned as I joined him, Bruno head-butting my friend until he gave him some love, "I screwed up."

"More than sleeping with a murder victim?" I sighed, more because I hadn't meant to say that out loud and felt guilty about it.

He nodded, wincing anxiety tightening his handsome face. "I told Allie I'd never met Sunny before," he said. "I might not have been one hundred percent honest about that."

And, just when I thought I could write off my conflict with her as a one-off. "Come on in," I said, dragging myself to my feet. "Let's get a beer and figure out what you're going to do to make sure she doesn't arrest you for being an idiot."

# CHAPTER SIXTEEN

I called Allie. Of course, I did. She arrived despite the early hour looking like she'd still been up, which I knew she had. Her classic bouts of insomnia almost guaranteed she'd been looking for a reason not to pretend she was trying to sleep. She'd told me her sleep issues were a holdover from her days in LA working all hours on homicide cases, but I had no doubt there was a solid background of some kind of PTSD adding its own little flavor of the month to her inability to get more than an hour or two at a time.

My dad might have died young, but I knew enough cops during my time in the forensics lab—

and dated a few—that I knew trauma sourced stress when I ran into it.

Allie accepted the beer I handed her the moment she walked through my door with a stoic expression and nod for Jasper, sitting quietly with her long legs crossed, looking casual in her t-shirt and cut-offs, flipflops a reminder I needed to paint my toes again since hers looked freshly groomed and mine were a notable disaster. While she didn't look the part so much in civvies, there was always something distinctly authoritative about Allie Crown that had even the charismatic Jasper Dunlop stumbling over words and apologizing as he filled us both in on his unintended untruth.

Starting by showing us both his social media from six months prior and a picture of himself and the victim smiling over drinks, faces flushed, from the dancefloor of Off Key.

"We *had* met," he said, dropping his phone into his lap while Allie sipped and stared over the lip of her beer. "I just didn't remember until I came across that pic tonight."

"By met," I said, knowing my dry wit was lost on him, if not on Allie, "you mean…?"

He wrinkled his tanned nose, shrugging. "I don't kiss and tell, Becks." Then laughed. "Yeah, okay, fine," he said when I snorted in response. "With you guys I do. She stayed the night at my place if that's what you're implying." His expression turned serious again however when Allie showed no sign of amusement. "I swear, it was only one night, and she was gone the next morning. It's why I didn't remember."

Six months wasn't that long ago, but it was an age for someone like him, so apparently Allie was fine with letting that pass.

"I know you didn't kill her," she said. "You can relax, champ."

He did, slumping down into my recliner, bare feet up on my coffee table, look of relief on his handsome face. "I don't think she remembered me either," he said. Almost sounded sad.

"Poor Jasper," I said. "Bit of a blow to the ego, there, is it?"

He shrugged then, grinned and took a drink of his own beer. "I'm pretty memorable, Becks."

That finally roused humor from Allie as both of us laughed out loud. Jasper didn't take offense at all, though he did sigh as he peeled at the label on his bottle.

"A shame," he said. "She was about to sign on Pine Pen next week."

Allie perked at that, as did I. "Pinehill Peninsula?" That strip of land had been for sale for as long as I'd lived here and while that was only six months, it was a long time for a property on the

Key. Likely because the owners were asking for an astronomical amount.

"I guess they found a spot then," I said, thinking of her and her friends and how their dream would likely die with Sunny.

Jasper shot me a strange look. "They?"

"The sisterhood." I didn't mean to eyeroll. Maybe I was jealous, because how cool would it be to have friends like that? Then again, Sunny and her little posse weren't all they seemed and certainly had their flaws.

Jasper shook his head, frowning. "Sunny was buying it solo," he said. "I should know. I'm the agent on the deal."

The fact Jasper now had his real estate license and hadn't told me was a conversation for another time. But I did have an exasperated question for him.

"When did she have time to hire you?" I was pretty sure I already knew.

"The night she… you know." He shrugged.

"And you still didn't remember her." Amazing.

Jasper didn't seem concerned with his memory lapse, even if I was.

Allie and I exchanged a look as I sat back with a smirk despite his truly despotic attitude.

"Well now," I said, saluting the chief with my beer. "Sounds to me like the queen bee was building a hive without her little workers."

"And could be an excellent motive for murder." Allie saluted back. Then sighed deeply before sitting forward, elbows on her knees, balancing her beer between her hands as it dangled between them. "I just don't have enough to prove it."

"What else did she tell you?" I prodded Jasper with one foot and with my words while Allie watched him with slitted eyes. "Since she trusted you enough to sell her property, it had to be more than pillow talk."

He seemed uncomfortable but nodded. "I guess she's dead now, so any kind of agent-client privilege is gone with her."

Allie reached out and flicked his big toe with her thumb and index finger. "That's not even a real thing, Jas," she said. "Spill."

"Just that she made tons of cash from her prenup," he said. "Bragged about making a killing off her ex, taking him for a full ride." Nice. "That her so-called friends were idiots." Wow, Sunny had real class. "Something about their divorces not being airtight."

Well, we knew that much now. "Because Chrissy told," I said.

He shook his head, earnest. "She said she made sure she was the first one so that her ex was the first to cheat, with one of the girls. That way if it did come out that they'd arranged everything Sunny would be protected by saying Chrissy was lying to protect Melrose. She knew her friend was in love with him."

Allie stared at Jasper for a long moment before casually reaching over and smacking his leg so hard he jumped and yelped at the contact. I highly doubt she hurt him, but she definitely startled the two of us.

Still deadpan, she tilted her head, blonde ponytail falling over her shoulder to dangle across the mouth of her beer. "And you kept all of this information from me why?"

Now, he may not have been the brightest bulb in the bunch, but Jasper knew quiet condemnation when he heard it. He winced, shrugged, sighed before opening his mouth, obviously to apologize. As Allie waved off his answer.

"Just don't." She stared down at her beer before polishing it off in a long swig, setting it down with a thud on the coffee table. "Okay, so she set up Chrissy, is that what you're saying?"

"Chrissy said she'd always had a thing for Melrose." At least I shared what I learned, sheesh.

Allie nodded, chewing her bottom lip now as she squinted at nothing. "Clever, really, though if Chrissy found out?"

"You saw the footage from the turtle cam?" I sat

forward myself. "I couldn't be sure, but it looked like Chrissy had her sisterhood purse with her."

Allie's attention returned to me. "Carter sent the final images with comparisons to the strap of Sunny's bag," she said. "Perfect match."

"And the last person seen with her—at least by a camera and that we know of—was Chrissy." Certainly wasn't looking very good.

"Someone who'd been orchestrated by a sociopath to take a fall so Sunny could get what she wanted." Allie stood up, taking her empty bottle with her as she strode around me and Jasper, heading for the kitchen. I heard the soft clatter of the bottle sliding into the waiting box before the chief returned to stand in the doorway, arms crossed over her narrow chest, backlit by the brighter light of the kitchen. "And someone who told me she'd left when the other women did and that was the last she'd seen of Sunny." A definite lie. "A someone who first said she'd thrown her purse away, then claimed to have lost it that night." Yikes. I waited for Allie to wrap up, knowing she'd already made up her mind, likely before this conversation, but had enough now to make an arrest and hand things over to the state boys. "I already have officers searching garbage bins along the main strip just in case she was dumb enough to dump it. But now I'm thinking I need to search her hotel room again. If she found out Sunny set her up on purpose, there may be evidence of that on her phone or computer. And that would be more than enough circumstantial evidence to move forward, even if I don't have the official murder weapon and the footage from the beach isn't conclusive." She dropped her arms to her sides, nodding to me. "Thanks, Becks. I guess I'll go pay her a visit right now."

# CHAPTER SEVENTEEN

I topped up a customer's coffee, the man barely looking up from the chat he was having with his three friends over breakfast as Florida sunshine beamed into the dining room at Low Key. Not that I minded being ignored by the four golf enthusiasts—impossible to miss from their logoed shirts, ball caps and garishly annoying pants that might have made them look like individuals if they weren't all trying so hard—as I filled in for Juliette over the breakfast rush. The yawn that finally made it past my defenses lived behind my raised hand as I turned from the window booth and headed for the main counter to refill my coffee pot, waving to the pair of women who tried to flag me down on the way.

The fact I'd been up most of the night with Jasper before my friend finally left meant an epic level of weariness since I'd been burning my particular candle at both ends for a few days now. And while it wasn't Juliette's fault I'd forgotten she'd asked me to sub in so she could go to her mother's doctor appointment in Key West, a bubble of resentment nevertheless encompassed my day manager, Jasper, the murder victim and those annoying women still snapping their fingers in my direction. Oh, and the golf dudebros because...

I didn't like their pants.

Don't get me wrong, I loved my place and did what needed doing because it was my place. And no matter how tired I was or how irritating the customers at times, there was literally nowhere else I'd rather be. So, the mild complaining and groaning whine I allowed myself at my lack of sleep and being forced to sling java at 8AM was a minor inconvenience I'd get over before too long.

Just as soon as the nasty woman with the perfect bob stopped glaring at me like I'd offended her because I didn't come to her beck and call, *Karen*, right this freaking *second*.

Inhale, exhale, set the possibility of murder aside with the coffee pot.

Fortunately, the server got to her first, which meant I wasn't going to have a nasty review on the website. Or, at least, not as nasty, because with her type, who even knew? I was in a position, however, to spot the familiar three women I'd come to wish would find somewhere else to hang out as they entered Low Key. Big sunglasses seemed today's necessity, Hannah Chang's so oversized they blocked out the majority of her face.

I waved off the hostess and greeted them personally, though I'm pretty sure the smile I forced into existence had an edge to it. "Good morning," I said. "Table for three?"

Nina nodded to me, sighing deeply as she stripped off her sunnies and gave me a wry smile. Bloodshot eyes squinted into the brightness of the dining room's interior as she winced. "Somewhere quiet?"

Naturally, one of the servers took that moment to drop a tray on the floor, the crash so loud everyone jumped. It wasn't just Nina who flinched, Latoya groaning while she pressed one hand to her forehead, manicured nails longer than anyone's had the right to be—especially for a cosmetic surgeon. As for Hannah, she swayed, skin vaguely green, when she clutched for Nina's hand.

"Right this way." I spun and marched off, a slightly mean streak in me celebrating the fact that while I was tired? They were about as hungover as I could have foreseen and hoped their suffering carried on a little while longer.

Petty? You bet. I was in a mood, so no judging.

It was pretty obvious by the way the tiny therapist sank into her chair, falling sideways as she did and needing help to get settled, that she was still tipsy from the night before. Nina and Latoya at least seemed on the far side of it, though when I set the three menus down, one of my servers joining us with a perky smile that made me feel old, I heard them instantly order Bloody Marys all around.

"I know," Nina said as I frankly stared, eyes widening at their condition and terrible life choices adding insult to alcohol. "But we've all received bad news this morning and I don't think any of us are willing to face the day sober just yet."

Hannah burst into tears, covering her face—giant sunglasses still in place—with both hands while Latoya rubbed her shoulder, free hand supporting her chin on fist.

"We've all had our prenups challenged," the doctor said, though she seemed resigned to it, as did Nina. "We're being sued." Only Hannah appeared devastated, but she was still drunk, so who knew how she'd react when she finally sobered up? Besides, from what I'd learned over the years, the people who gave the mental health advice were sometimes the ones in the most need of it themselves. No doubt Hannah's present state had been helped along by some medications not normally recommended be mixed with booze for breakfast.

Not my problem and I was totally over it, thanks.

"That's too bad," I said, about as far as I was willing to go at this point. Until I looked up and took note of Melrose Lewis standing at the entry, staring at the three women with the kind of intensity expected from a sharpshooter prepping to take out his targets. I almost left them to him, since Allie didn't need me poking my nose in any further, except that protective big sisterness I'd never been able to shake showed up when he pushed past one of my young servers and came to a halt at the women's table.

Now, maybe if he'd been polite to the tiny teenager with her bouncy curls in a ponytail instead of treating her like she didn't exist, I might have walked away and let him have at it. But my staff deserved better, even if these women didn't, so I held my ground and made sure, as Melrose stopped and smirked at the trio of suffering divorcees, that he knew he wasn't welcome in this part of my establishment, either.

## CHAPTER EIGHTEEN

It took him a moment to shed his self-satisfaction and meet my gaze, finally doing so when I leaned into him, grim expression obvious, even to someone like him. He took a half step back as I tilted my head, pot of coffee held at chest height, maybe casual, maybe a perfect weapon.

"You cause one speck of trouble," I hissed at him, "and you're out. Got me?"

Melrose shrugged, looking uncomfortable suddenly. "I'm here for breakfast."

"If I say so," I said, gesturing with the pot. "But we might be full. Depends on how the next few minutes go."

I'd clearly doused the bitterly happy fire of his vengeful approach, and he didn't seem to want to accept it. But he nodded, shrugged, before addressing Nina.

"Have you seen Chrissy? I need to talk to her." The biting satisfaction was back, but he wasn't making a scene, so I let it unfold.

"I have no idea why you think I'd know," Nina said, droll and completely undercutting his attempt to dominate her, the entrepreneur sitting back, crossing her arms over her chest, expression flat and cold.

"She told me everything," he said, leaning into the table, intensity a hiss until he shot me a look. Clearly, he read mine correctly, because he instantly straightened again, sullen anger simmering but quiet again. "I'm challenging Sunny's estate. I'm going to win and your husbands," he pointed at the three of them, dropping his hand when I held up the coffee pot, "are going to follow suit."

"You might want to hold off on celebrating," I said, copying Nina's tone exactly as Melrose glared at me. "Your witness is in police custody and I'm not sure how believable she'll be to a judge and jury if she's convicted of Sunny's murder."

They all gaped at me. Whoops, I really was tired because no way I would have let that cat leap out of the bag otherwise. I knew better than to flap my lips about a case, inwardly wincing and hoping Allie would assume they found out from local scuttlebutt. Even as I resigned myself to confess to her the moment I had the chance.

It was Hannah Chang who laughed, snorting and crying all at once as she clutched at the table with both hands. Before jerking off her sunglasses and smiling up at Melrose with a cracked and crazed expression on her face. "Good luck with that," she said. "But if Becks is right? You and the rest of them," the ex's, I guessed, "can kiss any kind of reversal goodbye." She threw her head back and laughed like this was the best joke she'd ever heard.

While Nina and Latoya both broke into smiles of their own.

Melrose spluttered, red-faced now, clearly thrown by this new state of affairs. When Nina flicked her hand at him, dismissing him, he almost lost it. I had to physically place myself between him and the table to keep him from leaping at her, seeing the signs and knowing what was coming a moment before he could act. No way was he causing a stink in my restaurant. Like it or not, he'd played a hand that might not play out the way he wanted.

"I'm afraid we're all full," I said then. "Maybe try the diner on Parrot Key. They might have a table open." The next Key over was only a short drive, but it wasn't breakfast he was after. I just needed an excuse to get him out of my place.

It worked, though I doubted my suggestion had anything to do with his departure. It certainly didn't help the women's laughter chased him to the door, however. They weren't getting away with stirring the pot either. When I spun to hiss at them to settle down, they did so but with reluctance.

I left them to their celebration, part of me hoping Allie found evidence Chrissy was innocent because suddenly I wasn't all that keen on those three getting away with what they'd done. I did note, as I delivered a plate of food to a regular, that Melrose Lewis hadn't left, but stood just outside the door, talking with some heat to the Charleston homicide detective who'd been lingering. Thompson Clark nodded but didn't comment as Melrose visibly rambled on, the pair making way for customers but staying in full view. I almost stormed the door to drive them off, when Melrose tossed his hands and left, Thompson watching him go before he turned and entered Low Key.

Again, I waved off the hostess, seating him personally at a small two-seater near the bathroom. He took the place graciously, along with the menu, though I noted he seemed to be watching the women again.

Irked me, yes it did. Why was he still in town? If he'd been here for Sunny, she was dead. He could go now. Yes, my attitude was far from gracious as I poured a coffee he hadn't ordered.

"How's the case going?" I moved to purposely block his view, Thompson glancing up at me with surprise.

"I'm sure Chief Crown has it all well in hand." He sipped the drink I'd poured, flashed a smile. "Great coffee. I'll have the Low Key Breakfast, thanks."

I took his menu and my leave, sighing as I glanced back and noted he'd pulled out his phone and now ignored the laughing women now into their second round of Bloody Marys.

Juliette hurried in, freeing me from my servitude. Her flustered thanks over the trouble had my attitude shifting.

"How's your mom?" My day manager was a gem and there was no way I'd take out my bad mood on her under any circumstance.

"Fine, fine," Juliette assured me, dark eyes wide and round cheeks flushed as she dabbed at the moisture on her upper lip, slipping into her apron and taking the coffee pot from my hand. "Sorry about this, Becks."

"Not at all," I said. "Anything you need. If you want to take the rest of the morning…"

She shook her head, squeezing my hand with her own strong one, flashing a smile. "You already do too much," she said, humbling me with that single statement. "None of us have told you, Becks, but we were worried when you bought this place." Juliette huffed a sigh, beaming at me then, dimples showing in her pale cheeks not designed for the Florida heat but adorable, nonetheless. "I have to say, we were all so relieved when we realized how wonderful you are." Um, thanks. Blushing. "Now, git." She swatted my hand. "I've got this."

I watched her hustle away with a smile on my face, feeling better at last. Sure, someone died at my bar two nights ago. That wasn't fun. And okay, three drunk women brought drama into my place on several occasions, but that was just life, right? The crazies came and went, hopefully, but this?

This was home.

I took time to finish some paperwork, knowing it was either this morning while I was already here (okay, fine then) or take it home with me (no, thank you) because it was either sort out the month's expense sheets or face the wrath of my bookkeeper. I'd just wrapped up collating costs—who knew there was so much freaking data entry to handle?—and was heading for the exit when the three women I'd hoped were gone by now stood and made their way toward the doors.

At the exact time I did.

That meant I followed their cab down Fancy Street, the main thoroughfare through town and took note as their ride pulled into the hotel that several police cars were present and that Allie stood behind her truck, talking with an officer who held something in his hands.

I almost kept driving and really should have. Except, for some reason, my hands disobeyed my mind's orders and I found myself pulling into the parking lot, climbing out and joining the fun as the women exited their cab to find out what the chief was up to.

Allie wasn't there for them, however, gesturing to one of her officers who held a plastic bag. He turned and headed for his cruiser and open trunk, impossible to miss the signatory purse resting inside said plastic zipper bag. I was close enough to him as he passed that I caught sight of the embroidered crown on the top edge, while Allie's voice interrupted the slew of garbled questions the now tipsy trio threw in her direction.

"Yes," the chief said, clearly in response to their demands, "you're correct. We found Chrissy Younger's purse in her room after all. Forensics will test it." Her gaze lifted to me as I arched my eyebrows at her, keeping my distance while she finished. "If I have any further questions, I'll ask.

For now, if you three will please return to your rooms," she wrinkled her nose, "and sober up, I'll be asking your lawyers to join us for a final interview." She strode past them, pausing next to me, sliding her sunglasses into place. "Not that I need to question them again," she said, voice low. "Good call on Chrissy. She stuffed that," she jabbed her thumb over her shoulder at the officer who'd secured the bag into his trunk, "under her bed, crammed between the frame and mattress. If I hadn't known to look..." she shrugged. "Whatever the case, there are a few blonde hairs in the chain." Well now. "So, DNA will tell us if they're Sunny Thicker's or not." She nodded to me. "Regardless, I have all five purses now, one of which is the murder weapon." Allie headed for her truck while I glanced back at the three women hovering in the parking lot, staring after the departing chief themselves.

Maybe it had finally sunk in? Ex-friend or not, it was looking a lot like Chrissy Younger was the murderer and despite the fact her guilt would mean the three might be off the hook with their ex-husbands, they seemed less willing to laugh about it now than they were before.

## CHAPTER NINETEEN

Bruno was perched on the front step when I arrived home, his wandering ways begun even before I left myself that morning. I offered him a deep scritch to his furry face before letting him inside, topping up his food bowl while I paced my kitchen, a tablespoon of peanut butter smeared on a chopped apple the extent of my late breakfast as I tried to shed the stress of the last few days.

Failed miserably. Something kept nagging me and I couldn't figure out what. So many puzzle pieces swirled in my head, tugging at my memories, reminding me I might be a restaurant and bar owner now, but I spent a large chunk of my adult life helping cops solve crimes. That part of me wasn't so willing to retire to a Florida key and shut up forever.

Someone knocked on my door, distracting me from the spiral I found myself in, Bruno whuffing a deep breath while I checked out who my visitor might be. The sight of Valentine Ortega had me staring and frowning while I eased open the door and looked him up and down.

He held out both hands, expression a little sad and devoid of threat, while Bruno stepped out onto the porch and gave him a solid sniffing over. When the big dog sat on his haunches and grinned up at the maintenance man, Valentine's hand immediately reached out to pat the dog.

Made him all right in Bruno's books and, frankly, mine too.

"I'm sorry to bother you," he said, nodding to me, swallowing visibly, dabbing at his forehead with a faded green handkerchief he tugged from one back pocket, still stroking Bruno's ear while he wiped the sweat from his face. "Is this a bad time?"

I shook my head, chewing the last of my apple, leaning into the post supporting the overhang of my patio. "Sorry about the other day," I said and meaning it. "You all finished up with Allie?"

He bobbed a nod, tucking the cloth away again, offering a small, nervous smile. "She cleared me," he said. Gestured at me. "I hear that's thanks to you and some proof you found I told the truth."

The video footage. I nodded myself. "Happy to help," I said. Waited while he shuffled his feet, Valentine looking down at Bruno while the dog happily wagged his tail and leaned into the man's touch.

"I'm a cook," he finally blurted before I could prod him. He met my eyes, his own hopeful and anxious at the same time. "When I was in Charleston, I mean. Went to school to be a chef but didn't finish. But I worked in two amazing restaurants, and I learned a lot."

"And now you're working maintenance at a golf course." Now his visit made sense.

"No one wants to take a chance on an ex-con," Valentine said, leaving it hanging.

Right. "You're looking for a job?" Of course, he was.

"I have references," he said in a rush, though he shook his head then. "They're old, I know. That theft rap put me away for ten years." Valentine exhaled deeply, looking out over the water in my backyard, not so much resentful as he was sad. "But they'd recommend me, and I'm happy to do a trial or whatever you want." No one deserved to look that desperate to do what they loved. And in that moment, as I connected my own selfish dots and how I'd left my life behind to pursue my passion, I made a decision I knew I'd never regret no matter what.

"Check in with Juliette once the lunch rush is over," I said, the glowing joy that burst across the man's face followed by a "whoop!" that made Bruno bark and stand, spinning in a happy doggy circle in response. I grinned back, waving off Valentine's excitement as he grasped for my hand and shook it vigorously between his. "She's the final word on the floor," I told him. "And Marta is for the kitchen. But you get those two on your side and you're in."

He bobbed endless nods as he backed away, face wreathed in smiles. "You're a queen, Ms. Hogan," he said as he hurried off, waving. "A queen!"

That had me chuckling as I turned to go back inside. Stopped. Stared down at Bruno with a scowl as something clicked. And headed back inside to my laptop and the need to satisfy my curiosity's niggling doubts.

It didn't take long to confirm what my subconscious had been trying to tell me. Nor to dig up who it was Sunny worked with all those years ago. That her past connection to her killer tied it all together in a nice, neat bow. Or to come to the conclusion that Allie was wrong and that I now knew who the killer was.

I just needed concrete proof as to why.

You're wondering why I didn't call her and run this by her, aren't you? In my defense, I was a) really freaking tired and b) had too much training for my own good when it came to connecting dots and c) had my father's sense of right and wrong that rarely meant I sat on the sidelines while d) I wanted to be sure I was correct before I accused someone of murder and e) embarrassed myself in front of someone I really liked and admired and had already irritated once in two days.

Yeah. That's a lot of reasons. That was my mind on a good day. And why I drove across town to the small motel near the exit to the Overseas Highway, Bruno stretching out in the back seat for his nap while I parked outside the office door. Had a room number in short order, the suspect's car missing from the spot out front. I parked down the lot a ways, knowing my Jeep's wrap stood out but hoping to be in and out before anyone was the wiser. Picked the lock on the door—thanks, Dad— and slipped inside in a hurry, closing it behind me before turning to look around the little room.

Noted the occupant had mostly packed, suitcase standing near the messy bed, a bag of garbage on the floor near the door drawing my eye. Weird. Who took their garbage with them? Unless…

Easy enough to open it, to use the edges of the

plastic to prevent contamination from my own touch, note the contents, now not unexpected, the evidence wound around the broken chain that had once been attached to the signature purse with the embroidery stitched into the upper corner. The purse with the dollar sign.

For an accountant.

Just like the star was for the entrepreneur, the caduceus for the doctor. The yin/yang for the therapist.

And the crown for the queen of them all.

Which meant, as I examined the murder weapon—it had to be, right?—I knew I was dead-on, if you'll pardon the pun, and that Chrissy Younger was innocent.

Her purse had killed Sunny Thicker. But I didn't believe she'd been holding it when it choked her friend's life away.

# CHAPTER TWENTY

As I stood over the garbage bag that had tried to hide the broken chain strap in question, I scowled at the evidence at my feet. This didn't prove anything conclusively, actually. If I was going to be honest, it just pointed even more strongly in Chrissy's direction. Except, if she had killed Sunny, how did her purse strap end up here? Wait a minute. Were the straps on the crown purse both intact? Carter had confirmed they had Sunny's DNA on them because they were attached to Sunny's purse. Allie had Chrissy's real purse with the obvious gaps where this strap had been. Did she miss that detail? Unless... I nudged the bag and realized the truth. There were two straps in there.

The killer thought of everything. Or thought they did.

Because both of these chains had long, blonde hairs wound around them. Which meant whoever planned to throw this evidence away knew planting Sunny's purse would frame Chrissy for the murder. He knew about the strap and obviously knew better than to leave the other one intact. Clever. And yet, so many questions remained. But they weren't for me to gain answers to. The fact remained, there was only one reason the man who rented this room want to hide these chains. And why he'd planted Sunny's in Chrissy's room. Because he killed the lawyer and messed up the bags, not knowing each woman had her own embroidered symbol and that he'd planted the wrong purse. Possibly without realizing he'd broken the strap in the first place.

I bent to gather the garbage bag in my hand at the exact moment the door slammed into me, pushing me forward onto my knees with a startled yelp. I twisted, landing on my butt and looking up in shock—I was shocked? Really? Idiot—to stare down the looming form of the real killer, a gun held steady in his hand as Thompson Clark closed the door behind him.

What, you thought it was Melrose?

"I was going to throw those," he pointed at the bag with the straps inside, "over the edge of the highway and let the ocean have them." The homicide detective waved at me with his gun, gesturing for me to back away from the evidence he'd been hiding. I scuttled away on my hands and feet like a wayward crab, though he didn't give me time to get up, pinning me against the small table under the television as his shoe scooted the trash out of my reach. "How'd you figure it out?"

I leveraged my feet under me but didn't stand, holding out one hand toward him. "Valentine told me," I said. "Or, at least, his situation did."

Thompson swore softly, shook his head. "Of all the damned luck," he said. "And of all the stupid places for her to decide to settle, it had to be in his path." Thompson sighed then, shrugged, a weary set to his shoulders settling in. "It's my own fault, you know."

"You loved her." That much was obvious. Thompson scowled but didn't argue.

"I loved her for a long time," he said, running his free hand through his short hair, excess of silver shining in the light. "I thought she loved me, too."

"What happened, Thompson?" I slowly stood, waiting for him to pull the trigger any second as I straightened, relieved he simply watched me right myself, gun unwavering, expression sad and thoughtful.

"She told me we couldn't be together until after the final divorce." So, he knew about the pact? "That once Hannah's was done, we could be together, and no one would know." He finally wavered, looking around the little room as if surprised to find himself there. "I came down here to meet her, surprise her. She said she was buying the property herself, that the girls were out of it."

"You found out they joined her," I said. "That must have hurt."

He met my eyes again, his brimming with agony. "She had to keep up appearances," he said in a tone that was clearly meant to reassure himself, not me. "That's why she left with that clown." Jasper.

"You were the friend who picked her up." Why hadn't Jasper told us that? Would have pointed us in a totally different direction. Allie, I meant. Except I was in the middle of it now, wasn't I?

Thompson nodded. "I couldn't stand the idea of her with him, so I followed them after they left the hotel. Tracked her cell phone." He didn't seem embarrassed by that. "She said the girls couldn't see us leave together. They'd know. It might throw off the whole plan. But when I was about to drop her off at the hotel again, she made me stop the car, got out. Said she wanted to find another drink."

His scowl said there had been more than that to the conversation. Likely angry words involved.

But now I knew how she ended up back at the bar despite being kicked out at closing time. She must have been drunk enough she forgot Off Key was closed.

"The plan to buy the land here, for the two of you to be together," I said. "Except she never intended for you to be together, did she?"

Thompson stared at me, mute and trembling now. "I confronted her," he said. "That night."

The night he killed her. "You followed her back to the bar."

He nodded, licked his lips. "You have to understand, I'd loved her for decades. I knew her when we were teenagers." Yes, I'd uncovered that easily enough, followed the trail back to their hometown where the local paper identified them as king and queen of prom. Where Sunny's delusions of being a reigning monarch were cemented, I guess.

"Is that why you falsified evidence for her in Valentine Ortega's case?" Because when I'd followed their trail back to high school, it had been from a certain time and place. Namely Charleston eleven years ago and the case that sent an innocent man to prison.

Thompson didn't argue. Sounded sad when he

spoke. "I would have done anything for her. And I did, you're right." He sank to the bed, still holding the gun on me but clearly distressed and distracted. "She called me one night, said she'd messed up, that evidence against him had been destroyed and it was her fault. That she'd be fired or worse if the truth came out. So, I planted what she said she'd destroyed." His shrug seemed inconsequential. "I believed her, that he was guilty. I trusted her."

"Except all you did was plant evidence against an innocent man," I said.

Thompson's jaw tightened, eyes narrowing as he retook his feet. Challenging him wasn't my smartest move, apparently.

"It doesn't matter now," he said.

"It does," I fired back with the only weapon I had. I was in this to win this, so either I kept him off balance or he shot me or both. Either way, he was confessing to what he'd done if it killed me. Gulp. "You sent someone to prison for ten years, Thompson."

He shook his head then, pacing back toward the door, between me and any possibility of flight. Not that I'd make it far with his gun aimed at me, but there had at least been a glimmer of hope. "I did it for her," he whispered, choked and hoarse. Before the gun snapped sideways in his hands.

"What happened?" That was the only piece I

didn't have.

Thompson barked a laugh, bitter, furious, broken. "She tried to blackmail me," he said, red rage in every word. "Told me she'd kept the evidence I'd falsified, that she'd had me do it so she'd have something to hold over my head. She wanted me to…" he trailed off, coughed softly, looked suddenly sick. "She wanted me to kill Melrose." She… well now. "He was sniffing around, knew about the pact, heard about it from Chrissy. She was going to turn me in and ruin me if I didn't kill her ex-husband and shut him up." He exhaled sharply, shock crossing his face, like talking about it made it real, suddenly. "She was here six months ago, saw Valentine. And hatched this plan to get me here, to get Melrose here." He blinked through tears now trickling down his cheeks. "She betrayed me, and I loved her." Thompson's face contorted, free hand fisting to punch his own thigh hard enough he'd be bruised from it. "I saw her fight with Chrissy at the bar. They were both drunk." He slashed through the air with that fist now a cutting-edge open hand. "Heard her tell Chrissy she'd ruined everything, that Sunny had it handled, had a cop in her back pocket, was going to get rid of all opposition and that Chrissy was next." He choked on that. "Chrissy left. Abandoned her purse, threw it at

Sunny, said the sisterhood was a lie. I almost walked away then and there. Except." He cleared his throat, voice warbling and cracking. "Melrose showed up. And she kissed him." I flinched myself at that betrayal. "She had a story for everyone, you know that? She told him she'd planned everything, set the girls up. Told him she'd done it for *him*. And he believed her." Thompson doubled over, breathing ragged a moment before he pulled himself together. "He almost bought it, the fool. But stormed off when he realized she was playing him. She laughed at him. I heard her laughing as he stormed away." Thompson's eyes pleaded for understanding. "I had enough. When Melrose was gone, I confronted Sunny. We fought." He wept openly now, ugly crying. "I grabbed the nearest thing I could, Chrissy's purse. I just grabbed it." He lifted that free hand, a claw forming, eyes glazed and far away as he relived what he'd done even as he gave it voice. "I wrapped the chain around her neck and…"

And pulled.

# CHAPTER TWENTY-ONE

My only priority was getting the gun away from him at that point. With his confession in hand, there wasn't anything else I really needed. Aside from not getting shot, that was.

Thing is, Thompson wasn't as done with me as I was with him. And my big plan to escape and get Allie or hand over the evidence and save the day seemed to have turned into a life-threatening situation I really wasn't prepared for. Sure, I'd worked with the police for many years investigating crimes and digging into evidence. But actually confronting the bad guys? Not exactly my wheelhouse.

That meant I had to improvise by keeping him talking while my brain desperately sought a way to get out of this mess I'd put myself in. And that meant asking questions. Or prodding him when prodding was a terrible idea.

"You took the wrong purse with you," I said. "You thought it was Sunny's that you used to kill her. But it was Chrissy's."

His face contorted as he scowled at the gun in his hand, mind far away. If only the rest of him would follow suit, but no such luck. "They were both on the ground, spilled over. Chrissy dropped hers, kicked Sunny's. I took the closest one. Dropped it after I choked her." He shook now, sweating despite the full-blast air conditioning that chilled my flesh as much as the goosebumps of fear rising and fading with the steady wash of adrenaline surges I could time to the wave of the gun. "I grabbed it again when I left, but I took the wrong one." Thompson's free fist hit his thigh again with that self-punishing thud. He was more out of control than the steady grip on his gun showed, though how he managed to keep it level while the rest of him trembled with emotion I had no idea. Obviously, his years as a cop served him well. Too bad breaking the law had taken over. "I grabbed Sunny's wallet and phone, the broken strap. Hoped whoever found her would think she'd been robbed."

"You avoided all the cameras," I said, hating that my gaze continually bobbed back and forth between the barrel of the gun and the handle of the door. Thompson didn't seem to notice, swaying where he stood, the weapon not moving as though his trigger hand had somehow detached from the grim reality of what he'd done.

"I had no idea about the purses," he said then. "Put the one I took in Chrissy's room, hid it under the mattress. Why did it take the chief so long to find it?" Clearly, he'd been in agony over the missed evidence and couldn't do anything about it.

"But it was Sunny's purse," I said.

"I realized that after the fact," he nodded, chewing at his bottom lip, free hand now running over his stubbled cheek with a harsh rasp, the scent of rank sweat reaching me thanks to the spinning fan on the air conditioner unit. Fear tainted him inside and out. "It wasn't until I got back here that I realized the strap wasn't broken and that I'd made a terrible mistake. I should have been long gone." The answer to why he lingered, then. "I had to risk going back into her room, tore off the chain." He gestured at the bag with the two chains inside. "You know, I've been a cop a long time. I always thought it would be easy to cover up a crime. But it's harder than it looks." He wiped at his trembling lips, smearing tears away with a shaking sigh. "It's so simple to make one mistake that will ruin everything."

"You're a cop," I reminded him, knowing my judgment came through. "You should have turned yourself in." My dad would be rolling in his grave.

He shook his head, barely but acknowledgement of my presence despite what I said, like he didn't hear it at all, and probably for the best. "I almost got caught. Thought I was home free when I heard Crown finally found the bag. When she arrested her." He blinked slowly, dazed. "It would have worked. Your chief assumed that Chrissy stole Sunny's purse." Wait, did the gun drop just a little? It did. I drew a slow and shaking breath of my own, trying to stay level, calm, while a ping of hope he might get distracted enough to give me a shot—no pun intended, I swear—at escape a real possibility. If I could keep him talking and distracted by what he'd done.

Except I realized my mistake when his gaze snapped to me at last, and he fixed me with a grim expression that was all business and even more murderous. "I didn't take you for the nosy type," he said. "What clued you in?"

He didn't need to know my dad had been a cop or that I worked forensics. Let him think I was just some bar owner who didn't know better. "The embroidery on the bags," I said. "They all had their own symbol. When I ran into Allie at the hotel, I saw the bag with the crown on it and realized it was Sunny's, not Chrissy's."

"You could have told the chief," he said, squinting at me now, confused and even more dangerous because he was thinking about me and my fate rather than what he'd done. The opposite of what I wanted.

"I should have," I said. Took a chance I could spin the story back to him. "You could have left both bags. You very well would have gotten away with it if you'd just left it alone. Chrissy would have been the prime suspect."

"You weren't there," he snarled then. Shrugged. "You're probably right, though. I wasn't thinking straight. All I could focus on was that Chrissy had motive. No one knew I helped Sunny with Valentine's case. I'm an idiot."

Um, he was a murderer, but I wasn't pressing the point.

Clearly my attempt to deflect back to what he'd done wasn't working, because Thompson seemed to pull himself together, nodding to me and then the bag on the floor at my feet, gesturing with the gun. "Now I have three things to dispose of on my drive north," he said. "The ocean will get the chain straps and the alligators on the mainland will make short work of you." Before I could protest or offer any reason why he should let me go—because he definitely needed to let me go, thanks—I found myself exiting the room with him behind me, his quick circle to my side as he grabbed my arm with his free hand allowing him to jab his gun into my back. With the hastily retrieved garbage bag fisted in one hand, I stumbled over the threshold and out into the bright sunshine, mind desperate for a way to escape but knowing I was so far out of luck at this point, it would take a miracle for me to survive.

He'd parked his car down the row of spots, close enough to my Jeep he must have been forewarned of my presence. Now who was the idiot? Oh, right, already knew I was guilty of that. As he dragged me to a halt at the driver's door, I had one thought and one thought only. I had to alert help to the fact I was in danger. But that would only put someone else in harm's way. But I knew if I got in that driver's seat and sat behind the wheel, I was a dead woman, and no one would ever find my body.

I had to do something.

Turned out, I didn't need to, because miracles sometimes came in large, brindle bundles that leaped from nowhere with snarls of savage fury and body slammed gunmen to the ground with their massive mutt enthusiasm.

I'd totally forgotten Bruno was in the back seat of the Jeep, but he hadn't forgotten me and whatever instincts drove the dog I'd adopted, he certainly had a nose for trouble. Namely, when I was in it.

Thompson's shock lasted longer than mine. It was the only reason I got the upper hand. The moment he hit the ground, breath whooshing out of his lungs, the gun skittering out of his grasp as the dog went for his throat, I pounced on the discarded weapon and turned it on the homicide detective.

Who tried to lunge for me, only to be pinned by the giant dog who growled his warning that Thompson finally took seriously. Two hundred and forty pounds of mastiff mix baring his fangs can have that influence on someone.

"Good boy, Bruno," I said.

Maybe it was just me, but I swear the dog grinned.

# CHAPTER TWENTY-TWO

I set a bottle of beer in front of Allie while Jasper headed to the stage with the karaoke equipment, the chief watching over the rim of her fresh bottle as our mutual friend did what he did best and charmed the crowd with his arrival.

When she tried to pay me, I waved off her cash, shaking my head. "This one's on me," I said, wiping the bar with my rag while Pika served the short line that was Sunday night at Off Key. We'd been testing different events on the quietest night of the week but closing down at 10PM meant there was a limit to the number of customers I could attract.

Back to worrying about my business instead of murder? You better believe it.

"You don't owe me anything," Allie said.

I shrugged, leaning into the bar. "Our hard-working police chief deserves a free beer now and then." She saluted me with it, grinning. "Especially when said police chief arrives just in time to keep my dog from tearing a man's throat out." I turned and looked down at Bruno where he'd curled up on his bed, snoozing and totally unaware—and uncaring—that I was talking about him.

"He's my hero," Allie said. "You're freaking lucky, you know that, right?" Real fear passed over her face, though she hid it well, clearing her throat, the memory of her squealing into the parking lot, the tires of her truck spinning gravel in a bullet-like shed of shrapnel still fresh in my mind, as was her grim expression when she leaped out of the still running vehicle with her gun leveled at Thompson. Alerted by a rapid text I'd sent in a shaking hand, bringing her running so fast I knew she'd broken a dozen of her own laws to get to me.

I looked away, cheeks heating. "I should have told you what I found," I said. "I'm sorry, Allie."

She set her bottle on the bar, the sound of Jasper's amplified voice calling people to come up and pick a song a moment's distraction before she spoke. "You heard our four friends are all being sued by their exes?"

Nice of her to change the subject to something a bit less embarrassingly stupid on my behalf, though not on the part of the ladies in question. "I did," I said. I'd heard as much directly from Nina this morning before the three friends—and their ex-friend—all departed the Key at the same time, if separately. Turned out Chrissy was in as much trouble as they were and the sisterhood was no longer a thing. Every woman for herself had a sad ring to it.

"It's a shame," I said. Waved off her obvious protest. "Not that they're being sued. They deserve it." Melrose Lewis might not have been a murderer, but he wasn't a good person, either. Then again, Sunny was a piece of work herself, so maybe they all earned what they got. "I'm mean the sisterhood thing." Still made me whimsical for some reason, nostalgic for nicer, kinder times with people who cared enough about one another they wanted to support and love each other until their last breath.

Sheesh, where did that come from? I just needed a date or something.

"Boss?" I turned as Valentine Ortega appeared at the door to the bar, smiling at me, a small carton in his hands, held tight to the front of his apron as he bobbed a nod at Allie. "Chief."

"Hey, Valentine," Allie raised her beer to him while I smiled at my new favorite cook.

"You need something?" He shook his head as I spoke, hesitantly holding out the cardboard container.

"Marta wanted you to try this," he said, blushing deep red, bushy eyebrows coming together as I took the offering. "She thought. You might want. For the menu." He spun then and fled, hurrying back to the kitchen door while I popped open the top and moaned at the heavenly scent of sweet butter and cinnamon that wafted from inside.

I shared the delightfully golden-brown churros, their perfectly formed spears caked in sugar with Allie, handing her a fork, offering one to Pika whose eyes rolled in raptures at the flavor. While I was already a fan of the dessert, whatever extra ingredient Valentine added, the extra kick of spice had me double dipping in the icing on the side.

"Good call there," Allie said, taking a second bite while I beamed.

"I guess something went right in all this," I said. "I told Valentine he needs to sue the state of South Carolina for wrongful conviction." While I was a cop's kid and was part of the system for a long time, I still believed in accountability and hoped he'd follow through.

"Careful," Allie winked over her fork. "If he

gets a settlement and opens his own place, you'll have a run for your money." I hadn't thought of that and know it didn't say much for my character I winced. Even as the chief laughed. "I'm kidding."

I shot her a crooked smile to cover my worry. "You passed Thompson Clark off to state already?"

She nodded at that, setting down her fork and returning her attention to her beer while Pika freed the carton from the two of us and inhaled the rest in three quick bites.

"He was arraigned today," she said. "Plead guilty."

No surprise there.

I spotted Dr. Carter Wilson before Allie did, the chief grinning when I quickly looked away, though she simply waved to the handsome doctor as he sat next to her, his sea-green eyes meeting mine, delicious face all the more attractive for that sweet smile.

"Next round's on me," he said. "Congratulations on closing the case," he nodded to Allie, "and not dying before I can take you out for a coffee." That was a bit more on the wryly accusatory side, though about the fact we hadn't gone out yet or that I'd put myself in deadly danger I wasn't sure.

Hopefully the former. And maybe I could confirm that.

My phone vibrated, a text from Mom making

my heart lurch. *Great news, honey. Gray wants to have the wedding on Canary Key!*

Dear God. Just what I needed. Glanced up at Carter who watched with a raised eyebrow. And took a chance because what was life without taking chances when your baby brother was getting married before you?

I tossed my cloth to Pika and leaned over the bar while Allie stood and left, heading for a table near the dancefloor, a couple of locals calling her name and waving her over. Carter watched her go in silence, though it was obvious from his careful expression he knew darned well why she'd exited. When he turned back, I smiled at him and felt my heart pitter-pat sufficiently at his returned grin I threw caution to the wind at last.

"Speaking of not dying and coffee," I said, "you owe me a date." His eyebrows rose, but his smile widened. "How about right now?"

# OFF KEY'S TEQUILA *Sunrise*

1 ½ ounce tequila (silver preferred)
¼ cup cranberry cocktail
½ cup orange juice (fresh squeezed)
¾ ounce grenadine syrup
1 cherry and 1 twist of orange

Fill tall glass with ice. Add tequila and orange juice. Add cranberry then drizzle grenadine down the side of the glass across the back of a spoon to allow to settle on the bottom. Add garnishes to rim and serve.

According to bartenders, ordering a Tequila Sunrise says you are in the mood to party. Tequila is a happy, endorphin-releasing alcohol that can make you the life of the evening. However, if you order your tequila this way, it's likely you're out to get drunk without the harsh reality of drinking it straight. Fun, cheerful and lacking in any pretention, a Tequila Sunrise goes down way too easy, so drink responsibly!

Looking for more **Becks Hogan?** Book two, *Mojit-Oh-No!*
is coming soon!

# AUTHOR NOTES

## MY DARLING READER:

I hope you've enjoyed this first book in the **Canary Key Cozy Mysteries** as much as I have. Becks came to me a few months ago, her dream of owning a bar on the beach too tempting a storyline to ignore for long. She's already whispering to me about Allie's past, more about Bruno, her own family and, of course, the handsome and delicious Carter Wilson. I already know there are at least twelve more books ahead, so stay tuned!

Now that I've wrapped this book, I'm on to a cozy novella for Petal Morgan, included in a new anthology coming in June. **Mysteries, Midsummer Sun and Murders** is on preorder right now, so go grab a copy so you're the first to find out what our favorite deception specialist is up to in *The High Tide Deception*.

I'm also working on the next two brand-new first in series. *The Curse in the Carousel Horse* (March) is available now for preorder if you're curious. I can't wait to introduce you to the next series, **Finders Keepers Cozy Mysteries**. You'll get to see the next three books of **Georgia Drake's** series (I'm already working on *Dead of Night*, *Dead Ringer* and *Ding Dong Dead*) as well as the next in **Fiona Fleming's Fleming Investigations Cozy Mysteries,** coming in April.

Stay with me, darlings. There's so much more to come.

Best,
Patti

# ABOUT THE AUTHOR

Everything you need to know about me is in this one statement: I've wanted to be a writer since I was a little girl, and now I'm doing it. How cool is that, being able to follow your dream and make it reality? I've tried everything from university to college, graduating the second with a journalism diploma (I sucked at telling real stories), am an enthusiastic member of an all-girl improv troupe (if you've never tried it, I highly recommend making things up as you go along as often as possible) and I get to teach and perform with an amazing group of women I adore. I've even been in a Celtic girl band (some of our stuff is on YouTube!) and was an independent film maker (go check out the Lovely Witches Club at **https://lovelywitchesclub.com**). My life has been one creative thing after another—all leading me here, to writing books for a living.

Now with multiple series in happy publication, I live on beautiful and magical Prince Edward Island (I know you've heard of Anne of Green Gables) with my multitude of pets.

I love-love-love hearing from you! You can reach me (and I promise I'll message back) at patti@pattilarsen.com. And if you're eager for your next dose of Patti Larsen books (usually about one release a month) come join my mailing list! All the best up and coming, giveaways, contests and, of course, my observations on the world (aren't you just dying to know what I think about everything?) all in one place: **https://bit.ly/PattiLarsenEmail.**

Last—but not least!—I hope you enjoyed what you read! Your happiness is my happiness. And I'd love to hear just what you thought. A review where you found this book would mean the world to me—reviews feed writers more than you will ever know. So, loved it (or not so much), your honest review would make my day. Thank you!